MW01170516

Because You Hurt

Written by Charles "Fox" Champion

Publishing by Fox Knight Publishing

Story Copyright © Charles 'Fox' Champion
Characters; are Copyright © Charles 'Fox' Champion
All rights reserved

Writer: Charles 'Fox' Champion
Editor: Brigid Weldon-Obando
Illustrations: Charles 'Fox' Champion,

Any reproduction, in part or in whole, of this story, its images, characters, or any other contents of this book without the express written permission of the copyright owners above. The unauthorized reproduction, in part or in whole, of this story will be prosecuted to the full extent of the law. This includes but is not limited to physical, digital, and/or any other form of distribution or development of this story, for reproduction or distribution.

Any characters, places, names and situations portrayed in this story are based in a fictional content and do not represent any actual people, places or events. Any resemblance to anyone or anything living or dead, in the present or past, is not intended any harm to the person, place or thing that may have been used in this story. All others are purely coincidental.

Prologue

An old farmer's legs were on either side of the large tractor tire as he took his hand tool and tried to break the bolts loose. They fought his desired outcome; shaking the tractor with each tug, pull, and push.

"You sorry sons of bitch, get off of there," the farmer said, taking his rag and wiping his brow. Standing up, the farmer went back to his tractors tool box on the other side to grab a pipe to put on the end of his tire tool to give himself more leverage. What he had not noticed was the jack he had brought with him had inched to the edge of the stand.

"Where you at? I know you're around here somewhere," the farmer commented to himself.

As as truck drove by the tractor was nudged by the wind it generated, it started to tilt even more his way. His face went pale as the tractor pushed him back on his butt and the tire slipped into the drop of the road causing it to tip his way. Knowing his last moments were at hand he covered his face with his hands when something took hold of the straps of his overalls and yanked him out of harms way. He rolled a bit in the field of maze from the force used to move him. Leaning up from being on his stomach he saw the smoke that came off the tractor as its fluids leaked and hit the hot exhaust pipe.

From in front of him a hand reached down.

"Are you okay?" Asked a young man dressed in old blue jeans and a white t-shirt. Reaching up he took the mans hand and got to his feet.

"Yeah I'm fine son. Thank you,"

"My pleasure. Be more careful next time. I might not be around," was all the young man said as he started walking down the old farm market road again.

"What's your name son?" The farmer called out.

"Johnny," he said walking backwards to answer the farmer.

"I don't know if you need one, but I could use a hand. Mind giving me one?" The farmer added. His words pausing Johnny in his steps. Smiling, the young man nodded.

"Sure I can help you out," and with that he went back to the old man that was grabbing tools to get the tractor back up right. Looking at the tools Johnny stood next to him.

"I'm guessing it's done this before?" Johnny asked.

"Yeah the's old farm roads have them there sink holes or even a really large ditch that causes them to slide my tractors tire right off. And if it hits just right it flips every time. Ol' red here has fallen over at least five times," he explained patting his tractor's finder.

"Well lets get that pesky tire fixed first, get it on and we can flip it back up right so you can get back on the road. How's that?" Johnny asked.

"Sounds like a plan," With that the two men worked on fixing the bolt that had caused the rim to separate from the hub. Finding it had cracked, Johnny worked his magic with some thick and oversized washers he found on the ground after the farmers tractor had fallen over. They had obviously come from the farmer's tool box. Once they had the tire on they took the accompaniment of jacks and other devices from the tractor and started lifting it back up. Each time it started to threaten to slide both men would hope back as to not let it fall on them.

They worked deep into the night to get the tractor standing back up. Finally as it landed and the tire bounced a bit they dusted themselves off.

"Well guess that just about does it,"

"Alright, well I best get going"

"Whatcha in a hurry for son? I at least need to pay ya. Heck if you can stand staying around a bit I wouldn't mind having someone as handy as you around for a while," The farmer said. Johnny just looked down the road for a moment then back at the farmer.

"I think I could spare a little bit of time. Sure I'll work for you for now." He stated as he helped the old farmer get up on his tractor.

"Great, hope on back. Should be somewhere to stand back there and I'll get us on home. The misses is likely worried right about now. Especially since I haven't made it home to eat supper with her yet," The farmer explained.

"Well we must not keep her waiting then," Johnny said jumping up on the ball hitch on the back of the tractor. Flipping a few switches the tractor struggled to start at first then just like a rumbling beast it woke up. Turning on the single remaining headlight the farmer put it in gear and took off slowly.

"And away we go," the farmer called out.

Chapter 1

Hunted

He had been lost along a dirt road leading to anywhere, and nowhere at all, for days. How he got there was an interesting story, but not one he was willing to let distract his attentions at the moment as he pushed on. The trees along his path stretched high above him, so high he could not see the tips. Along one side the trees followed a cliff basin as high as what you would expect from the Grand Canyon. Looking up from time to time he got the feeling that someone was watching ... No! Stalking him. Considering all he had was his sturdy work boots, blue jeans, and a tee-shirt he didn't have much in the way of protection. Add in the fact he had a cellphone in a military like case, some car keys and a wallet he had nothing to fight back with. Looking down at his watch he thought to himself.

'Well at least when my phone runs out of battery I can still tell what time it is.' Pausing, he heard what sounded like a growl. His brows perked and his eyes widened. There was definitely something stalking him. Lowering his arm the time was not nearly as important as it once was. His pace quickened. Being surrounded by trees was not the best place to be if he was ambushed. He needed to get out from under them as quick as possible.

"Unless," he uttered out loud as his words continued in his head, "I climbed a tree. I bet whatever it is can't attack me there." With that he scrambled up the nearest tree. Getting a good distance off the ground he heard a scratching on the limb above him. Slowly looking up he saw human like figure that almost looked animal like, that he could not completely make out. The figure lifted it's leg as it was about to stomp on him, when an arrow hit the figure in the back from the side. Falling forward two more arrows whistled and hit the figure in the arm than another in the thigh. Without hesitating he reached out and grabbed the figure's foot. His grip on a knot of the tree began slipping. Looking down he saw two men with bows run up under them. They started to draw when he looked back up as he lost his grip and he and the figure fell towards the ground. Landing on the men he shook it off to find the man he landed on was dead: Likely due to breaking his fall when he careened into him. The other one was out cold from the force of her body making contact. Again his eyes went wide. She?! He thought. The creature he saved was a she. Taking another look at the men they landed on they were no normal humans. Both bared sharp tipped ears and odd skin tone.

"What th' hell is going on?" he muttered to himself as he heard the creature cough and stir moaning in pain. Knowing it wouldn't be long before the, 'elf' as he would call them, woke up and was out to kill them again, he needed to move. Looking her over quickly he found she broke her arm in the fall compounded by the fact she had two arrows in it as well. Her leg was not much better as it was pierced through the thick of it. Grabbing her good arm he lifted her the best he could and started dragging her away from the spot. Her body weight was far greater than he had expected as they moved slowly. Not making it too far he noticed an opened field; perhaps that would give some running room along the edge of the tree line. Dragging her several miles along the edge of the field he stopped when he finally felt it was safe he nearly collapsed from exhaustion. All he could hear was the creature's moans and groans as he put her down. Her glare burned through his soul as if he was the one that hurt her. That didn't matter so much to him as he was still captivated with what she was. Never before had he seen anything like her.

Of course that was the real question was it not? Her head was like that of a big cat, say a jaguar. Body tight and slender but covered in fur from head to toe with brilliant colors of white, orange and black. Feet bent in a manner a kin to that of a cat. Even a tail swished in anger around her legs. Surely that was what she was. A cat. Very large and beautiful cat but a cat all the same. With apparently, a breast halfway hanging out. Which was honestly the only way he knew she was a she in the first place considering cats are not exactly know of those animals he can easily tell gender without a massive set of -- well I'm sure I don't have to state it again.

"Wow, you are one beautiful beastie aren't you?," he said admiring her beauty as a beast. Thinking to himself he probably should not say things like that out loud, but it was clear she did not speak his language.

"And I have no idea how I'm going to take care of you. You're too damn heavy to just trek to some near by city, not to mention the panic it would cause," he looked around trying to think on how he was going to help this poor soul.

"I'll just have to improvise. First things first." With it getting dark he knelt down to see exactly how bad the arrow was in her back since it was in the deepest. The others went through the skin and out the other side. The arrow entered in just behind her arm and ran across her shoulder blade and the tip poked out right next to her spine.

"That has got to come out," he said looking back at her. Lifting his brow he noticed she was drinking some kind of a strong smelling beverage. Likely alcohol. Snatching it from her hand she started to fight back only to groan and nearly double over. Breaking the tail of the arrow off he made sure the feathers were clear as he pushed her over on her stomach and started pouring the drink on the wound. She screamed loudly in great pain. Taking the harden case of his phone he knocked the arrow head through the skin. Then while still pouring he pulled the arrow through near the spine and free of her body as he poured the drink all over her back. Rolling her back over he helped sit her up against a tree as he noticed the strap to her outfit was ripped over her right shoulder.

"Huh, so that is why you had a tit hanging out. Here I was thinking you were just some kind of savage," he smirked as if she would get his joke. Obviously still mad about either the drink or the arrow being pulled, or even possibly both, she yelled a growling tone at him.

"I'm sure glad I can't understand a word you said," a sigh escaped his lips. Calming down she reached with her good arm over her shoulder to find the arrow gone. Wincing she looked down at her arm. Turning to him she lifted the flopping limb towards him. Was she actually communicating with him? Nodding her head at her arm then, look back at him it was clear. She was telling him to take the arrows out of her arm. It would not be as bad as the back as the arrows had broken during the fall just like the one in her leg. Still part of the shaft remained, and that was what he needed to remove. Taking a moment he noticed that the remaining arrow shafts were just long enough to splint her arm, but what would he use. His belt! But first he would need to pull the arrows. Walking around her feet where her tail began to curl between her legs he could tell she was preparing for pain. With a little hesitation he reached down and snatched out one of the shafts as she growled and hissed pulling her arm away. Then slowly presented her arm again. There was no doubt in his mind this cat was crazy. Shaking his head in disbelief at the situation he began to work that last shaft in her arm. This one would not be as smooth, for as soon as he touched it he could tell it cracked down the center making it want to split as he pulled it.

"That's not good," he said to no one in particular. Grabbing the two halves he found that if he pulled on the split from opposition sides it came free easier than if he tried to just pull it free like the last one. She growled again, but this time not as loud or hissed. With all the parts he needed he positioned the wood on each of three sides of her arm. Her brow creased on curiosity. Reaching down to his boots he started unlacing them. Taking the shoe lace in hand he wrapped it around her arm as she growled and hissed trying to push him away with her other arm. Once done he tied it off and let go. A much better choice than his belt. Rolling away she kept him in her sights as she looked her arm over.

"Heh, yeah your welcome," he scoffed at her reaction as he got to his knees. About to get up he watched her lift her injured leg at him and scoot on her butt towards him. Straddled between her legs he looked upon how she had positioned herself as she had all but placed her hips up against his feet so her other leg could be lifted high enough for him to remove the last arrow.

"You have got to be kidding me," was all he could say as he looked down at her leg to notice she was about to loose her modesty. Thrusting her hips to lift her leg in motioning him to get to work he sigh and sat back on his legs. The ones in the arm were one thing. This one in the leg was something else completely. Running his hand along her thigh he racked his brain trying to figure out what the best way to pull the arrow shaft out as there was almost nothing but stubs left on each end. Reaching back the cat grabbed the phone he had dropped after getting the arrow out of her back. Passing it to him, he looked down at it then at her. Maybe she had a pretty good idea. If he could only push one of the stubs far enough he can pull the arrow out all the way. Pressing the hard phone case towards the arrow stub of her inner thigh he was met with gritted teeth and no sound. Her breathing had all but stopped too. Her body leaned back and head arched away from him it was clear she was toughing through the pain. Little by little he exposed more and more of the arrow shaft as he tried to grip on the other side. Finally she looked back his way hissing and growling. That was more what he expected. Taking the tip of the corner of his phone he gave it one last hard push right into the tender meat finally giving himself enough to grab on to. Kicking him away with her other leg he rolled back on to his back side. Purring in sued as she scooted on her butt up to him again. Inching back he was met with her purring louder and scooting even closer. "Yep crazy," and so was he for helping her as she leaned forward again this time straddling her leg so she couldn't kick him again. Grabbing the arrow that was exposed it came out much easier now that it was able to be gripped. Arching her back and screaming she almost sounded human for a moment as he tossed away the arrow's remains.

"There," he said as he stood up and dodged her swinging at his leg with her arm.

"Ungrateful," covered in blood he turned and started walking away from her when he noticed she was chortling towards him. Was this talking? First it was hissing and growling, not chortling. What was going on with her? Shaking his head he figured it did not concern him anymore as he started walking again. This time a full on meow escaped her lips and as he turned to look back at her she purred again reaching out her arm like a child asking to be carried for.

"You have got to be kidding me," he thought to himself. Yet he still found himself walking back to her and lifting her into his arms as if a parent carrying an injured child.

"This is so wrong," he muttered. No matter what he couldn't carry her long as she was too heavy for him. Her sheer weight made him walk funny. That and the fact he tried his hardest to not cause her too much pain on her leg as how he carried her could not feel that good and each time he readjusted he was either grabbing right on her injury, or too close to her chest. But how else was he going to carry her? Piggyback? She would be in more pain then she was how he was carrying her as she would rub her leg against his side the whole time. Of course picking apart how he was carrying her would be the least of their worries if that remaining elf came after them.

"Ah, ta hell with it," he said as he put her down on her good leg and picked her up piggyback. As he lifted her she growled then bit the back of his neck. Out of instinct he swatted her nose over his back. Rubbing the spot she bit, he held on to her and continued walking. Carrying her like this was much better even though he knew he couldn't do it too long. She was still pretty heavy. That and they would have to wrap those wounds soon as well and get more alcohol or she would bleed out or get infected.

*****

His legs ached from the walking he had done. With no water for far longer than they should have it was taking its toll on him, and clearly taking its toll on her. Still riding piggyback her head lay upon his shoulder and her arms hung to her side. Huffing and puffing he knelt near a tree about to put her down when he heard the sound of rushing water. With a sudden burst of energy he lifted her up and started to where the sound was coming. Squeezing through the trees near then he found the water he was looking for. And there it was. Cold. Crisp. Beautiful water. Kneeling at a tree near the bank the cat stirred and winced to being set on the ground. Standing up he started towards the water only to have the back of his knee kicked out from under him. Her words urgent event without his understanding them. Standing up and brushing off his pants he glared with her for a moment. Before he could try again she swung at him a few times. Tripping he fell on his back. Shuffling in an odd on the ground waddle she fought with him as she covered him with her body to take hold of his head turning it towards the water. There on the other side he watched a deer drinking go to walk off. Wobbling and collapsing the deer went lifeless as the cat let him go. Groaning she rolled off of him giving him as stern look. She just saved his life. For his benefit or hers was still not clear. Sitting up the cat reached out to him. Getting to his feet he brushed himself off and took her hand positioning her on his back once more.

"I know you don't understand a damn thing I'm saying but if we don't get water soon we are going to die," he explained to her over his shoulder only to be met with a growling worded response.

"Yeah, that's what I thought you would say." Sighing and shaking his head a bit to his annoyance with it all. Itching the back of his neck for a moment where she bit him, he adjusted his grip on the cats leg and began walking. This time she did not fall asleep upon his shoulder like before. This creature that was so intent on not having his help now almost commanded him even if without words despite her obvious distain for him. 'That's alright,' he thought to himself. 'Two can play this game. I may have started helping you out of kindness, but I can follow your lead until I get where I'm going.' His motive was not as simple as in his head. The fact was man or beast he was not one to turn a blind eye to those who picked on others.

Tapping his left shoulder she pointed her claw tipped finger to a fruit dangling from a tree. It looked a lot like a watermelon but far smaller. More like the size of a soft ball. Making the gripping motion with her fingers he knew what she wanted. Pausing next to the tree he sighed almost ask if to wait for her to ask politely, then instead let go of her leg with one arm and plucked the fruit and handed it to her. She bit into the fruit as it dripped down his shoulder only to have her shove in his face. Turning sideways he tried to stop her only to have her cram it in his mouth when he opened it to talk. The shock caused him to drop her on her tail as she released a loud growl. Taking it from his mouth he was about to complain only to find it was almost as if his mouth had been met with a cup of water. The fruit was near hollow inside. She had just given him his answer to water. Tilting his head he pondered, "did she understand what I was saying?" Surely she could not. However he had made it clear he was thirsty back at the river. His posture soften as he now felt bad about his over reaction. Walking over to her he went to lift her again only to have his hand slapped and scratched away. Gripping his clawed hand in the other he watched it start bleeding before his eyes.

"What the hell?! I'm sorry okay!" Throwing up his hands in frustration. She ignored him and rolled to her good side stabilizing herself with the tree.

"Hey look I'm sorry I didn't..." He started as he tried to help her only to be shoved back with her words growling his way. He would not be able to live it down. The fact her tail swished violently behind her didn't help. Hanging his head he could only shake it with no other course of action. More to the point no course of action he could take to make it better. However, the more important question was it should he follow her? Or let her go upon her own way. Which was an ironic situation as he had just faced the same question when he and his wife broke up. Too many late nights out and not enough quality time together or something like that. He never really paid too much attention. There might have been something about wanting kids too, but again, he didn't really care. A little itch in the back of his mind nagged at him to follow her as he knew she was easy pickings for any elf that might come along.

"Shiiiiit!" He muttered as he jogged to catch up to her. The more he watched her struggle the worse he felt. Finally to make amends he took off his tee shirt leaving his tank top and jumped in front of her. He placed his hand on her chest to stop her forward motion.

"Stop for a second,"he said when he notice her facial expression before she looked down at his hand. Blushing he yanked his hand away quickly. Ripping up his shirt he didn't notice the mirth she had at his reaction.

"Look," he said as he took the strip of shirt and wrapped her arm in the cloth. She growled a few times to indicate the pain it caused. Finishing up he took another two strips from the cloth and made a sling for her arm. Making two more strips out of the remains he angled to her side and zipped his hand threw her legs from behind. Wrapping it quickly around her leg not noticing her facial expression as to how impersonal he was being. Not wanting to draw attention to herself, she said and did nothing other then tense up her muscles. He dismissed it all as if it was a reaction to the pain. Tying it off he stood back proud of what he should have done in the first place. Smiling he was met with a far sterner face than he had anticipated.

"What?"

There was not sound from her as she struggled to walk on. This puzzled him as yet again he had not found favor with her for his actions. Save it for later, he thought to himself as he followed. Surely he deserved what happened to him. These thoughts traveled with him the rest of their trip.

Chapter 2

Reasons

In the middle of a small clearing there was a cottage next to the most majestic waterfall. Its waters rolled down the wall of stones between the foliage that surrounded it. Covered in moss and bushes the cottage was clearly made of stone and wood. Which the cat apparently knew all too well as she walked into the structure as if she owned the place. Within the walls she helped herself to bandage wraps and other such medical items. He followed her into the cottage looking around at all the herbs and other type of medicinal purposes. While she worked he strolled around her place in awe. So many strange and different things he had never seen before. Picking a few them up he looked and felt them over as if to memorize the shape. All was well and good until he came face to face with an object covered in a sheet. Looking over his shoulder he took sight of her catching her still busy with whatever she was working on. Slowly he lifted the sheet from the dome like object only to drop it back and stumble backwards. Looking her direction again she did nothing. She had not noticed his reaction. Looking back at the dome he saw a dark brown almost red hue soak through the cloth. His heart raced in shock. All he could do was stare at the domed object and inch away slowly. This was something he would not talk about. Grunting and growling she motioned at him. It wasn't clear what it was but the motion of her arms almost looked like she wanted him to follow her. Glancing over at the domed object he silently walked after her cautiously. She on the other hand moved with purpose. Slung over her shoulder is a sack filled with all the stuff she had collected. It was not that far of a walk as she led him in her hobbled gate. The path they followed took them between bushes and brushes that was only wide enough for a single body.

It was well hidden that you had to know it existed to be able to follow it. Down the path he could see light starting to shine in front of her as she emerged into a small village. He followed her only to be suddenly grabbed on either side. To his left and right were more cats like her. Presenting their claws they held them to his throat as they turned and growled in the direct ion of the cat he was following. She gave a scoffing face to them. Behind her a much older cat walked up to her side looking her up and down stopping on each of her injuries.

"This is not going to be good," he said under his breath. No sooner he said those words the old cat spun his head around towards him. Rushing up on to his face the old cat gripped his chin and grumbled words to his face then gave a forceful push away. It was met with the two cats carrying him off to a stair way leading down into a stone structure that was underground. Fear started to grip him from head to toe as his life was in the hands of these creatures that did not seem so willing to be charitable at the moment. In the bottom of the structure there was a round holding cell with another body being held to the wall by chains. The body looked in their direction but said nothing. Grabbing some chains off the ground the two cats clasped them to his wrists and walked off. He wanted to yell for help of try to reason with them but he knew it was falling upon def ears. Sighing deeply he knew his fate had just turned for the worse.

"How are you going to get out of this one?" He asked of himself. From across the room the other figure in the in the room started talking. That must be Latin, he thought, no! French. But the more that he listened the more it was clear. That man across the room was not speaking English. Even the man across the way was noticing the lack of understanding. From nowhere the mans eyes began to glow as streams of energy slowly crept across the room to the new captive. Only a foot away from his face the cats came back in the room.

"Hey! Hey!! Come help me out here. Get this shit away from me!" he pleaded. One of the cats crossed his arms while the other just smirked. They wanted this to happen. Whatever it was it was something they planned. Those bastards, he thought. Backing up to the wall as far as he could go he closed his eyes and turned his head away as if it would help. It did not. Surge of excruciating pain covered his head and into his brain. This must be what a tumor feels like, he thought to himself. An affliction he lost his grandmother to, too long ago. Throbbing waves of his migrain caused his eyes to pulse with pain as it spread until suddenly it just stopped and everything became blurry as he opened his eyes. What just happened? Did that man across the room project a headache into his head? How is that even possible? Then the man spoke.

"Ugh, you are no elf. With that primitive and disgusting language of yours. I believe you are actually of a tongue worse than those worthless beasts," he man across the way was not making a friend in him anytime soon.

"Oh yeah now you speak," he said in reply to the man as he continued, "Who are you?"

"Sylocur. High elf shaman of..." he started only to be struck with a large stick by the nearest cat from a good distance away. "I'm apparently not allow to talk to you. Well not until they start asking you questions." the elf said.

"Yeah...right," was all he could reply only to hear the cats ask the elf a question. Sighing the elf turned towards him.

"So, that is what they are after. They want to know who you are? Basically what your name is or that your made of? I never can truly tell as their language is far more dynamic then it needs to be," Sylocur sarcastically quarried.

"Well thats kind of a smartass question. I'm a human obviously. And my name is Clarence Thied. But everyone calls me Cledis," he explained still a little insulted by the question in the first place. The elf leaned forward to where his face was visible. The shock upon is face told volumes.

"So you do exist. Ha! I thought Ragn..." again the elf was interrupted before he could finish the name. Immediately the cats wailed on the chained elf, while another unchained Cledis grabbing him by the neck with claws extended. The cat led him out of the dungeon of sorts and up to the surface where the older cat was waiting. Out of the pan and in to the fire, he thought to himself. Surly there was no way it could possibly get worse. On a stump in front of the old cat was a cloth over another dome like object and it was covered in red.

"No!" He started to panic as the last time he saw a cloth like that it was not a pleasant site. Closing his eyes he was dragged over to it and his hand was forced to touch the head under the cloth. A head. Peeking he looked upon the head of another cat. This was not the same head he saw in that female cat's place but still. Not something pleasant to see. Or smell. Taking his hand away the cat let go of it and the cloth was placed back on the head. Was the old cat smiling at him? He asked himself as the cats behind him let go of his neck. The female cat he had traveled with hobbled up slowly. The old cat and her conversed for a time before she motioned him like she did once before for him to follow. More and more he felt like some sort of toy. This was embarrassing, but necessary he thought. Perhaps he could have his chance to escape when they were all asleep for now he would just follow her and see what was to come. It was not far from where they had presented him the head under the cloth as a rather large makeshift hut was standing on the edge of the village. She pulled back the hide that was used as a door to reveal cats of all ages and sizes near emaciated. All of them, everyone, coughing or vomiting. The site was even more shocking than the head he had seen. Was this the site of an epidemic? Some kind of plague? She began to talk to him as if to have a conversation. Of course he understood none of it. Still she spoke. Then he heard the elf.

"We did that to them. She is tell you all wrong but. It's still amusing to hear how they describe the events," the elf told him.

"What? What did you do?"

"We poisoned them. Those filthy beast were in the way. Our new ruler wants them all wiped out. And that is were your world comes in. We can dispose of humans easy. Then take over and the resources will give us the edge to finally rid us of all cats," the elf said almost boastful. Cledus watched a large cat konk the elf over the head and he was out. Dragging him off they took him back to the layer they kept him. From his side the female cat grabbed his arm and started dragging him along. Stopping in front of her species equivalent of a child she patted her busted arm looking him in the face. Then she grabbed his head and turned it towards the child. Taking her finger she placed it on his eye as he closed it to her touch. Good thing he did as there was no telling what kind of dirt she could have on those pads of hers. Moving her finger from his eye to the body before him she tilted her head. Clearly she wanted him to look at the child.

"Fine," He said as he first pulled back the hide that was being used as a blanket. Placing his hand on the child's chest he felt the heat radiant from its body. Far too high if it was a human. Getting a second opinion he placed his wrist against the child's forehead only to jerk it back. That child would be brain dead at this rate. But there was no source of ice or water from all he could see around him. Turning to her he motioned as if drinking from a cup of water.

"Water. I need some water," he finally spoke. Turning she grabbed a large gourd like object that was very heavy and passed it to him. Popping the plug of wood he smelt it only to find it was not a pleasant smell.

"Damn that is no good," he uttered only to catch a glimpse of the same fruit she gave him when he was thirsty before. Seems she had uncovered it when she grabbed the gourd. Rushing over he grabbed it and walked back to her. Placing it to her mouth he waited for her to bite it. Instead she tried to turn her head away. Shaking his head he grabbed her lower jaw and opened her mouth shoving it in her mouth and clapping it to make it bite the fruit. Spitting she clearly was not happy. As soon as she saw him poor the fluids all over the child and place some in the child's mouth she knew what his intentions were. Growing wide eyes she ran out of the tent and came back with several other cats and more fruits. Coughing the child spit out the fluids. Turning and smiling at her, his smile turn to a frown as he knew they could not be there for a good reason. Grabbing his arm she moved him to the next patient and had her fellow cats bite the fruit and pass them to him. One by one he used up the fruits and the cats would leave and come back and form a line. before too long all of the sick cats were stirring again. Far from healed but closer to being alive than they had been for what was obviously a long time. What really puzzled him was the fact as soon as the cats were done he notice helping her was like a bother to them. Perhaps her people did not try to help the sick normally. If that was the case this must have been an extreme situation for them all to pull together. Sighing deeply the thought of what he had gotten himself into crossed his mind. Looking over at the female cat next to him he looked her up and down. He couldn't help but think there was something there worthing being interested in. She looked back at him with a slight purr emanating from her voice.

"Watur," she said lifting a fruit for him to take.

"You said water. It's pronounced 'water'," he corrected still greatly shocked. So the cats could learn his language. This was a good thing because most of the growls, clicks, chortles, and various other sounds they made he could never repeat. It was hard enough to learn Spanish more or less a whole new cat language. Taking the fruit from her with his right hand he presented his left hand.

"Cletus," he explained. She looked at his hand for a moment then that sour face he was use to came out. With that he was shot down and she walked away. Sighing out of frustration he knew it would take much longer than that to make a friend out of her. Looking down at the child he had started with earlier he spoke to them.

"I think you're the lucky one. At least you have others to connect with even if you are practically dead. Falling off balance he found himself being pulled along by the cat as she led him out of the tent and off down the path they had came into the village from. Making their way back to the little cottage he started to resist a bit as he knew what was under that cloth. Not knowing if the other cats where waiting in the trees to kill him he followed her in but made a mental note to give the head a wide birth. He practically stood in the door way as she shut the door behind them and walked down the hall taking off the sling he had made her. Stripping one article of clothing after another she came back into the room with nothing on and presented her arm.

"No. You can't take that off," he instructed. She gave it a small shake to draw his attention to it again. "No I will not," he added. She went to cut it off with her claws herself only to be stopped by him. "It will never heal if you take it off," his face showed the seriousness of his words. Looking at the arm again and then back at him she let it go. Reaching down between her legs she grabbed the cloth there and ripped it off tossing it on the table next to her and she walked out her front door.

"What tha heck is she doing?" he thought to himself. He watched as she walked over to the waterfall and started drenching herself in the water.

"Animals have no modesty at all," he muttered as he watched her bathe. Except he looked closer and the more he looked her body was not that far off from that of a humans. Sure it had the head of a leopard, and tail, even the feet bent like a cats. Toned and sleek she was a sight to see. He had to shake it off as if he kept looking at her like that the lines would beginning to blur. Turning and sitting down propped up against the house he just watched and waited for her to finish. Snatching up a blade of grass he started pulling it apart in an attempt to distract himself. Before he knew it she stood in front of him again. He had been so busy distracting himself he never saw her hobble over. Looking up he quickly blocked what he saw as she looked as much human from the front as she did from behind.

"Go put some damn clothes on!" he scoffed. Snatching the grass from his hand she tossed it down walked off into the cottage again swishing her tail violently behind her. Shaking his head he was going to wait till she came out but it bothered him too much that she just took the grass from his hand. Being a cat, more to the point big cat, she would have to eat meat if she was anything like the cats he knew of his own world. What right would she have to be upset with him about destroying the single blade of grass when she would kill and eat other animals. Bursting in the door he was met with her backside turned towards him.

"What was that all about? You can't tell me I did anything wrong by picking at that grass. Heck there are thousands of blades of grass out there," he argued only to have her turn towards him again. Protecting her modesty with his hands he placed them in front of his face to block her appearance. She started chattering at him in her language as she pushed him. Not expecting it he fell back on his back. In her hands she had a blade of grass she shook at him. Furious words flowed from her mouth as she tossed it back onto her table and pointed her finger at him.

"Nou, Nou!" she attempted to say. He knew what she meant even though she got it wrong. Those blades of grass apparently had more importance than he was aware of. What really stung though was the fact it came off more like a dog being corrected for leaving a puddle on the floor. Noticing during the conversation that she was trying to twist her broken arm, he got up off the floor and looked around on the table. Following his gaze then staring back at him, she was clearly puzzled. Finding a wide handled spoon he took it up along with a piece of wood and handed to her. Unwrapping her broken arm she hissed and started to growl before going silent. keeping her arm as straight as possible he took the spoon and placed the bowl in the palm of her hand and aimed the handle towards her elbow. Wrapping it around the palm and wrist he took the other stick and followed the bend of her elbow with it then held it there. Rolling the wrap around her arm over and over again he ran out of wrap half way up her forearm he was met with her handing him a wide super thin strap of leather more than enough in length to finish the job. The entire time he was wrapping her arm he tried to be as gentle as possible, receiving a purr from her with an occasional hiss when it hurt. In that moment he felt a bit of a connection that made him want to ask her questions. Opening his mouth just closed it again as it would have been no point.

"Whaught?" She asked amongst her purrs. Taken back it took him a moment to compose himself again.

"Why...do you have that head on that table there? And why doesn't it smell?" looking at the head she stopped purring. An extended silence passed between them for a moment before a tear rolled down her cheek. Turning back to him she began to stumble with the language she was trying to learn quickly.

"Hee...moi...mmm" her words stuck on something she knew not what to call it.

"Boyfriend?" he piped in.

"Nou,"

"Husband?"

"Nou,"

"Sister maybe?" For those words he received a slap on the arm and a glare. "Okay, okay, not sister. Geeze the way you were acting he was your brother," She replied to his words with an ever so slight nod of the head and almost winking of the eyes. This must be how they say yes. Looking over at the head again he could not believe she would have that on her table.

"Whun words yoo, touk buthah," She explained before continuing. "Ef eh' 'old buthah, buthah nou liv'. Wan byt...mmm," again she stumbled on her words. So instead she motioned as if to indicate all.

"So the head would come back to life and try to bite everyone," He translated, even though he was not sure how. "Your english stinks by the way." Shrugging her one good shoulder she just went back to watching what he was doing.

Finally finishing up he had wrapped her whole arm up to the middle of her upper arm. The spoon handle poked out the end near her elbow. She could no longer twist her wrist but now her arm had a chance to heal.

"There. All better. Don't take it off for six weeks. If you do it's not going to heal right," he explained.

"Et eal right," she said as she took a cup of ground up grass she had gotten on to him for and started drinking it in an almost paste form. The mixture smelt awful as it was worse than the smell of the most pungent weeds.

"What is that stuff?" he asked her making a disgusted face at it. She answered in her native tongue. Apparently she had no words he could understand to call it. Shrugging it off he watched her place it down then hand him a bucket with a sponge like object filled with a weird looking chemical. Nodding her head she looked at the blood stains on his clothing. Taking the hint he started to brush the stains down watching them almost melt away. Looking up presently surprised at the results he caught her slipping on a new outfit as if it was all normal to dress in front of him.

"Why do you do that? just strip and dress in front of me as if it's no big deal?" he asked.

"Ou nou us. Nou prublim," she said finishing up and turning around.

"Yeah, not you. No problem," Shaking his head was all he could do. Yes it was true he was not her kind but it didn't mean it didn't come off a bit bothering that she looked so much like a human woman that it made him a bit uncomfortable. Letting it pass she took his arm and pulled him along again. This time around back to a door like a cellar that he had not noticed before.

When she opened it he noticed meats being hung on ropes from a bar. Pointing to one of the meats she looked at him. Taking the hint he pulled the meat from the depths of the hold and held it for her to see. Closing the doors she took the meat in one arm and headed back inside her cottage. inside she went to another room deep in the back near where she had gotten dressed not long before. Laying it on the table she tried to rip off a patch of meat only to have it fight back. Seeing her struggle he placed a hand on the meat and held it while she pulled it free. Holding the strip in her palm she presented it to him. He grimaced at the groosum thought of eating meat without it being cooked. Not wanting to be rude he took it in his hand and looked at it. Giving a gentle push of his hand she indicated for him to eat it. No way he was going to eat this meat without cooking it first. Looking about he found a small area where she had built fires and took the meat over to the spot. Never once laying it down he used his free arm to build a fire until he realized he didn't have a lighter. Standing up sighed thinking he would have to save face and just eat it raw. Noticing something that shouldn't be on her table he grabbed the Bic lighter and started a flame. With the fire lit he grabbed a flat stone from the floor and laid it over the fire giving it time to warm up. She cautiously walked over looking puzzled at what he was doing. Only when he finally laid the meat upon the rock and it began to sizzle did she realize what he was doing. Shaking her head she went back to her meat and started pulling strips to eat for herself. She did not eat it fast however as his method of flipping it by grabbing it and turning end over end fascinated her. Finally ready he pulled the meat from the stone tossing it back and forth from hand to hand until he reached the table. Ripping it quickly in half he passed a piece to her and she started tossing it from hand to hand as well. Blowing at it he got the meat to were he could bare to hold it and took a bite. Her brows lifted. He intentionally ruined the meat so he could eat it. This was no elf she thought to herself. It did smell good. And she was as cats usually are. Curious. Sniffing it, the aroma waft into her nose causing a sensation that caused her mouth to water. Going wide eyes she was surprised as she looked at him who was already at the end of his meat and attempting to pull another strip to cool. Taking in a deep breath she closed her eyes and bit gently upon the meat as its juices flowed into her mouth. The amazing flavor was like nothing she had ever experienced before. He may not be an elf but he did know what tasted good. Standing from her spot she took her place beside him and observed how he cooked the meat. This was something she would want to do for herself someday. In the end that fire did more than just prepare the food they would eat, but provided the only light they had left as the night fell around them.

Chapter 3

Atrocity

Opening his eyes slowly he found himself sleeping on the floor of the cottage. Sitting up groggily he wiped his eyes. Sleep was something that alluded him that night. Who knew the cat people things would snore so loud. It was a kin to a chainsaw attacking a block of harden stone. Or put in simpler terms she purred and growled at the same time. That in itself was disturbing. Figuring he would let her sleep he stood upon unsteady legs as he made his way outside. Splashing water in his face should wake him a bit better he thought. Opening the door he turned the corner to find the cat knelt down splashing her face with water using her one good arm. She had the same idea apparently. Kneeling down next to her he glanced over to her.

"Morning," he said politely as he began splashing his face. Smirking she sat up looking back at him.

"Mooning," she tried to repeat his words.

"Mor...ning. You don't want to respond with 'mooning'. It's considered rude," he corrected.

"Mo..rn...ing," she tried again. Sitting he smiled at her.

"Much better," his words were interrupted as a snow flake fell between them. This was something that was amazing to him as where he came from snow was very rare. That and it didn't even feel cold enough to snow. However her face was not as amused. To her this could only mean one thing. The elves were attacking more than just them.

"What?"

"Dey hort..." she ended her words by patting the ground. His brows contorted inquisitively.

"They can do that? What tha hell are these...elves anyway? How can they have power over the Earth itself?" The idea was just beyond him.

"Evs av many puwers," she explained as she jumped to her feet. Before she could advance the both of them were thrown off balance by a quake that shook them off their footing. He fell forward dipping one arm into the water. She on the other hand tilted backwards and into the water with only her feet on the land. Quickly he grabbed her feet and dragged her out of the water till she was on the ground once more. Sitting up coughing out water she brushed the water off her face. Kneeling next to her he patted her back.

"You okay?" he asked looking at her with concern. Nodding was all she could do. Looking towards the village nearby he stared.

"That was really close. Felt like something hit the land or something," he explained.

"Need see lan. See it urt," she said trying to get to her feet. Taking her hand in his he cradled her back in his other and helped her up.

"You mean, we need to see if the village was damaged?" he corrected.

"es," she nodded and turned to the path to the village. A short padding of foot steps away they entered the village to find next to the stone structure the cats kept the elf in accompanied by another stone structure. More like concrete to be exact. He tilted his head and walked in front of the building that stood before him. He began to read the signs painted on the glass windows from what was left.

"Best cuts in Brooklyn," No sooner did he utter the words that a pudgy black man come stumbling out of the front door of the shop.

"Their all dead! Oh my god the earthquake killed my friends," the man said turning back to his shop falling to his knees covered in grayish dust.

"Whao whao, lets calm down. Is anyone else in there alive," Cletus said only to get an odd look in return.

"Don't kill me Mr. Terrorist. I promise I won't tell anyone, just let me live," the black man pleaded. It was ignored as Cletus ran past at the sound of moaning. Rushing through the door there were several people laying on the floor in the back of the shop. A few others were scattered on the floor near the door he had come in. Apparently they had tried to make a run for it and did not make it far. He reached down to find the first person was dead from the glass that had cut them fatally. Seeing the next person he grabbed an arm and started dragging them out of the building. They were far to heavy to lift up on his own.

"I don't know what your name is but I would suggest you get in here and help me!" he yelled to the other man just outside.

"Oh yeah right," the black man jumped to his feet and rush to Cletus' aid. Grabbing the victim's other arm they began to drag him free of the building just as the back half of the shop fell in on itself. Letting go of the mans arm Cletus left the rest to his help and the cat he had came with. All the other cats just watched from a distance. Running back to the back of the store as far as he could he found it was too late for many of the people there. Grabbing a slender woman that was not completely covered he lifted her to find her leg had been snapped off by the falling celling. Rushing her out of the building Cletus laid her on the ground next to the other victim.

"Oh snap!" said the black man before he fainted. His cat companion looked at him.

"We will deal with him later. Please stop her bleeding or she will die," he instructed before running back in. One after another he pulled five other people from the building. There were another three he could not get to due to the caved in roof. Cletus and the cat spent hours working on the people that were injured from the strange building that seemed to have crashed into the village. What was really puzzling him was the fact no other cats were helping at all. The old cat of the village that seemed to be an elder did nothing but just stand and stare at the going ons.

"Your people are real douchebag, you know that? They could at least help us here," Cletus scoffed.

"You Peope ar nou us. We elp us," she said in response.

"Then why are you helping me? Or them for that matter," he added curiously.

"You nou evs. Evs nou elp you. Mak you mor us, nou evs," Her words were clear even if the pronunciation was not. To him she might as well said the enemy of my enemy is my friend.

"Gee, thanks a lot," he ended as he focused on the rescue instead. Nodding her head to him she thought there was a moment of understanding. However that was farther from the truth. Cletus was more incline to let the cats rot with this elf trouble. The fact she was actually helping him, he could not fight with her about it currently. There were still lives to save.

******

Deep into the night it was her and him working to keep the lives they had saved stable. The black man had indeed woken up and passed out again a few more times before he was finally able to stay awake. Being all they could do had been done Cletus walked over and sat where the black man was sitting with his back to the victims.

"Hey, we lost three more of your friends. Just couldn't stop the bleeding," Cletus informed him only to be met with weeping. The gravity of the situation had finally hit him.

"I'm sorry man,..I...That was like my family," he said before starting another bout of weeping.

"Yeah," Cletus uttered only to go silent. What could he say to help? people died and when this man was away those man like cats just stood around and let them die. Looking over his shoulder he watched the female cat tending to the living and dead tenderly. As much as he was mad at her there was something that caught his attention. Something that was growing no matter how much he would want to deny it.

Cletus' thoughts were interrupted by the sound of one of the victims groaning. He was coming to.

"Tyronn?" the black man said as he ran over to the victim's side.

"Jabber? What in the hell just happened?" the injured man asked.

"Man, I don't know, allz I know is shit started shakin' and I got my black ass out of there as fast as possible,"

"I thought I saw a black streak," Chuckled Dyronn.

"You thought that was me, neaw that was," he paused to look around then pointed to the closest black furred cat he saw, "It was him." Even Dyronn didn't believe him.

"Now that is pretty low. Blaming it on tha only black cat in tha room," Dyronn pointed out as he winced to the pain he was feeling trying to move around.

"You...you didn't see? We ain't in no room. We out in tha sticks. Y'know the same ones that white boy over there might use on us later," Jabber again tossing the blame.

"You just donno when ta shut up do ya?" Dyronn commented before turning his attention to Cletus, "You'll have to forgive him. He was raised to have manners but ain't got no sense to use em."

"Hey!, Wah what are you doin' I thought you were my brotha?" Jabber whispered.

"Oh, I'm you're brotha alright, but I ain't about to pick a fight with someone because you actin' a fool," Dyronn replied turning on his stomach lifting himself off the ground. Without saying a word Cletus walked over and helped him to his feet then walked him to a log that was large enough to sit on.

"Really?! You just gonna help a brotha even though his brother is right here. Man if I only had half a mind,..." Jabber started to say only to cower away when Dyronn and Cletus looked back at him.

"I ain't time for that shit, just ain't got time," Dyronn muttered to no one in particular.

"Eh, it's what brothers do," Cletus said as he set Dyronn down.

"What? aw neaw, he ain't my brother, he's a brotha, but not my brother. Heh I would have killed him long time ago if he was," Dyronn corrected.

"Hey!" was all that could be heard from Jabber. Shaking his head Jabber turned around speaking to himself about being dissed only to find the very dark furred cat came over glaring at him intently as it crossed its arms. Turning to scamper over to the other humans he was looking over his shoulders causing him to trip and fall.

"Ah! They got me, go on without me Dyronn, just save yourself,"

"Get your butt up off tha ground and stop makin a fool of yourself," Dyronn told Jabber. Jumping to his feet and brushing himself off Jabber acted as if he had intended to fall.

"Em not whol'?" the cat with the broken arm asked of Dyronn.

"What tha?" was all he could respond with.

"She is wanting to know if he is missing a few bricks from his load. You know...mentally off," Cletus clarified.

"What did you say?" Dyronn asked of Cletus in a serious manner. "Don't you ever talk about my boy that way again..." he warned only to trail off in the middle of his own words. "But yea he does seem a little...Off." Cletus glanced over at the cat as she had pulled some kind of sharp object from her belt line. Placing his hand on her arm she barely flenched as she tucked it away once more.

"What is this?" Jabber asked.

"What is what?" Cletus answered truly unsure as to what he was referring to.

"Man, I've heard of jungle fever, hell I've even had some before but this. Man, this is something else. Y'know that jungle fever like that is only going to be called beastiality," Jabber added only to have the back of his head slapped by Dyronn.

"Whacha do that for?"

"Cause you a damn fool, now shut up for once in your life," Dyronn demanded the pouting Jabber.

"Yeah, I'm gettin' tired of hearin' you as well," said the woman laying on the ground. Leaning up she reached down to the missing leg rubbing. Standing Cletus started over to her only to have Jabber try to beat him to her only to trip and fall on his face. Reaching down Cletus helped her sit all the way up.

"What happen' to my leg?" she asked.

"As far as I could tell it was taken off when the roof fell in on you. Which is really lucky thing too," Cletus added as she took her arm over his shoulders and helped her hop to the log.

"How's dat lucky? I lost my leg,"

"Because everyone else the roof fell on died," Cletus added as he sat her down next to Dyronn.

"Dangit, I was gonna help her and you saw it," Jabber cried.

"That's cold dawg, she just woke up. Ya could have told her that later," Dyronn commented as the woman next to him started to cry. Dyronn continued he comforted her, "So'k Ragina."

"Hey she could be back in tha wreckage. Ooo, Ragina Wreckage, Ha ha! caus' that's were we found her. Ha ha!" again Jabber was not making the others happy.

"That's cold," Dyronn called out.

"Shut up Jeremy!" Ragina spat at him.

"Seriously come on," Cletus added.

"I ain't listen' ta you white boy. Heck you're probably named Cletus or something like that wit your white wife beater. So just hush it," Jabber lashed out. Cletus blushed as the cat next to him stood up again she reached for her blade again as Cletus pipped up.

"Actually, my name is Max," He knew this was going to cause a problem as he had already told the cat his name was Cletus. She turned to glare at him when he tried to respond.

"Why are you looking at me like that. Your people have been keeping me as a prisoner when they aren't treating me like a slave," Realizing what he had said he blushed even more as he could hear the comments of what right he had to say that. The cat turned to walk away. He reached for only to have her turn on her heals slashing across his body from shoulder to shoulder cutting a straight line across. Stumbling back he watched the front of his shirt cut open and blood start rolling down his skin.

"Woah! she got you good. Whachu get for tryin' to make a slavery comment," Jabber jabbed.

"Did they force you..." Dyronn started only to have been interrupted by Max.

"Yeah, they did," All he could do was watch the cat walk away. "And she was the only one that was decent."

"Why you talkin' to him like that? He some kind of redneck. You do remember what happened in that movie Deliverance right?" Jabber commented.

"Look I don't know you very well, but if you have made friends with that cat, Ya probably should fix it," Dyronn added.

"It's probably the only way we gonna get outta here," Ragina had made a good point.

"Yeah cause you ain't gettin' none of my sweet asHHHH!" Jabber yelled as he was smacked by Ragina.

"Shut up and sit down!" the anger of a black woman was something that not even a black man dare fight against. Almost in tears Jabber went to complete silence and sat down with a thunk.

"Heh, doesn't seem to matter where they come from, never mess with a woman," Max mused wiping his blood with his fingers as he looked at his hand. Looking back to where the cat had disappeared into path leading to her cottage. Looking back at the three before he left he nodded receiving two nods in return. Jabber of course still pouting. Dashing off he chased after the cat. Zipping back and forth to try and avoid the limbs and bushes that extended over the path it took him moments to emerge from the path and see her headed for the water. Looking over at him she glared and continued to the water. He started to run towards her only to get half way before she turned to glare at him again. Behind her a deer got spooked and started to run off. It had been drinking from the water seconds before. Getting only a step or two the deer fell to the ground and started its death throes. His eyes went wide at the sight. Noticing his face she turned around to see the target of his attentions. Turning to her gaze at the deer then ran to the edge of the water and pulled a strip of leather from her belt line dipping it in the water. The strip of leather turned a purplish red. Out of anger she punched the ground. Walking up to her side he looked down at the strip.

"What's wrong?" he asked of her considering to kneel only to know she was still not happy with him so thought better than to do so.

"Make dea' can nou drink," she explained.

"How? How is that even possible?" She did not answer his question but stood up tossing the strip of leather into the water as far as she could throw it. Turning to him she punched him directly in the chest. The impact was so ferocious it nearly knocked the breath out of him.

"You say nam'. You nou nam'. Why?" Even though he listened to each and every one of her words he caught the fact that she had said one of her words perfectly. Pulling his attentions back to the matter at hand he stood his ground as her face came nose to nose with his own. Only an inch or so taller than himself she was very intimidating.

"Because you tried to kill me. I had no idea what you had planned for me. First I'm tossed in with that pointy eared freak. Then you force me to help with all the sick. Which I've noticed that whole tent is missing and all its patients. So how was I to know you wouldn't do the same to me?" he rebutted.

"You nou 'ave happen befo' you gav nam'," She pointed out.

"Yeah...yeah you are right. But nothing you did or said made me want to trust you then," neither said a word as the cat looked down and back a way a bit. Perhaps she saw his point, he thought.

"You 'eal arm," she pointed out as she touched the side of her arm. Gently she gave a half blinking of her eyes and nodding of her head. Was this her way of saying thank you? It was not exactly what he had expected. Getting in close she nudged the bottom of his chin with the bridge of her muzzle. The sound of a soft purr emanated from her once more. Without thinking about it he closed his eyes and wrapped his arms around her hugging her. Suddenly stopping her purr she took a moment before she closed her eyes and began to purr again hugging with her one arm in return. Before long she found her head laying upon his shoulder nuzzling him a bit. This caused him to smile. With all her ferocious hissing and scratching she was nothing more than a big pussycat at heart.

"That is the loudest purr I have ever heard in my life," Said Jabbers voice from behind them. Quickly pulling from the embrace they both looked back at the three that gazed upon them. No sooner they had Jabber was being slapped again.

"Don't chu ever know when to shut up?" Ragina questioned. Interrupting with urgency Dyronn motioned back to the village.

"There is some crazy mess gonna on back there. Some weird pointy eared dude came in burnin' down all the buildin' and stuff."

"We need them to stay here. They can't help us could they use your cottage?" Max asked the cat. All she could do was nod her head. Thankful of her response without thinking he cupped both sides of her face and kissed her on the lips. "Thank you!" Running over he helped Ragina and Dyronn over to the cottage. The cat was still wide eye and in shock. Apparently she did not know what to think or do with the kiss as she had gripped in her hand the blade she was quick to always grab. The whole time Jabber was making off color remarks about him kissing the cat. No sooner that he got the three in the cottage he turned to her and motioned her to follow. They both ran back into the village to find intense fires raging all over the place. Cats of all kinds ran back and forth in the confusion. In the middle he noticed an elf directing the other elves around him. The elves were attacking both the structures and the cats. Not knowing where to start him and his cat friend fended off elf after elf from attacking the cats. Which all became worse as snow started to come down heavily. A piercing chill followed. In the middle of fighting off the elves Max turned to watch the elder cat walk up to the elf. Standing there amongst the chaos the elf and elder cat kissed passionately then walked off hand to hand. This was an odd site indeed but he didn't have time to worry about it as he went back to fighting off the elves only to see them retreat with the old cat and the elf that had left.

******

The elder cat held the elf in adoring eyes as they had stopped in a clearing just out of sight of the smoke and fire that was consuming the cat's village.

"I was worried I wouldn't see you anymore my dear," the cat uttered.

"You won't need to see me anymore," the elf explained.

"Wonderful. Does this mean we will finally go to start our own pride?" the cat asked.

"Not exactly," was all the elf said before shoving a long blade into the cat causing him to burst into a bluish green flame. With in the plumes the soul of the cat fought for freedom only to be drawn into the blade and the body fell like an empty husk bursting into ashes and floating away with the wind.

"Sir, seems that spell of deception worked perfectly. But did you really have to kiss that beast?" asked an elf.

"Yes. While an illusion my trick the eyes, the actions will trick the soul. At this point his entire tribe thinks he just betrayed him. Any that may survive will be too busy trying to track down the traitor to bother with us. Remember a cat's honor must come first. A breaking their trust clouds their mind," he explained with a wicked grin.

"Yes sir," the elf responded to his leader.

"Besides they will have disappeared from existence before they realize that they can never have their revenge," with those words the group walked on leaving the bits of the older cat's accessories and clothing to lay in waste. The leader elf smug in plans. He held his blade at waist high as he watched the cat's blood soak into the etchings upon the sides will it was gleaming clean again. Guiding it with his other hand he placed it back in it's sheath.

Chapter 4

Holocaust

They stood in the midst of the smoldering structures which were extinguished by the falling snow at how fast it was falling. The blood on Max's shoulders had froze into ice crystals. Everyone had fled to the winds. Only ones left was the cat with the broken arm and himself. They had saved many lives, and lost a few. Still the village was gone. They would probably have to leave as well as there was no drinkable source of water and the snow didn't seem to be leaving soon. Looking over at the cat they both shivered near violently. The only thing keeping them from falling victim of hypothermia was being active trying to stop the carnage. Tilting his head he motioned her back to her cottage.

"We need to move before we freeze to death," he suggested turning on his heels. Following suite she said nothing as she was close on his heels. Each leaf felt like razors as they hit his skin. His shirt was draped down around his waist. Finally free of the path the two made a b-line through the mounting snow to her door. A path barely visible lead back around the back of the cottage. Looking at each other she pulled her blade ready to attack as he rushed in the door with her behind him. Closing the door slowly they inched through the rooms to see if any elves had invaded. In the back room where the table was the three were chowing down on a slab of meat they had obviously pulled from her hold behind the house. Which would explain the path that led out. Taking a deep sigh he shook his head.

"We thought you guys had been attacked," He exclaimed.

"Neaw we was just hungry. Want sum?" Jabber asked as he flipped more meat on the grill. The fire below the meat was huge. Burning bright enough to light up the room and provide heat to combat the cold. Just shaking his head to the events Max turned to look at the cat only to find she had walked off. Sighing he just leaned agains the door ripping free the shirt he had once wore. Using it to wipe his wounds he was met with the stinging force of the cat pressing some kind of soaked cloth to his chest rubbing off the blood from one shoulder to another. He almost jumped out of his skin from how painful it was. Looking over at her he could tail she was trying to make up for cutting him in the first place. Reaching his arm over he placed it on her side.

"Thank you but it will be okay," he informed her. She nodded as she turned away carrying off the rag.

"Aww," Ragina pipped in.

"You too are jus' unbearably cute," Added Dyronn.

"It's creepy. They should get a room somewhere far far away from here," Jabber butted in.

"Now I know you ain't comin' up in here talking that shit,"

"Ragina's right. Wasn't you who said that, that white girl could have been a rabbid dog and you still wouldn't have cared caus' how much you love'd her?"

"I didn't say that!...Those were different times...Just eat ya meat," Jabber started to pout yet again. "here have some meat," he said passing it to Max.

"Thanks," was all max could say as he started to bite into it only to have the cat catch his hand and pull his hand to her lips taking a bit of meat. Then nodding for him to eat after her. Giving off a slight smirk he cautiously took a bit himself.

Shaking his head Dyronn commented, "Too damn cute, s'all I has ta say. Too damn cute." Max wanted to say something but instead he didn't say a word. Being friends with the cat was not necessarily a bad thing. However that was not what had his attentions. The cracking of something very large and very close was causing him to turn his head. Starting to turn he was met with the cat having passed the rest of the meat to him. Far from concerned about the meat he placed it down on a nearby flat surface to meet the cat passing him a new outfit to cover up like his shirt did. Not as clean of a design or hidden stitch but it did cover him well. Dawning it he was handed a fur to place over his shoulders that draped down his back as soon as his head popped out of the top of his shirt.

"Thank you," He said as she presented her back to him and over her shoulder held up another hide. Gently he covered her shoulders with it. Reaching up she pulled it together with her hand and headed for the door. Following suit he kept close to her as they pushed through the snow. Gazing up they both were met with the awe of the waterfall freezing but at the same time still flowing. The loud cracking was the base of the waterfall breaking free.

"GET OUT OF THE HOUSE NOW!!!" yelled Max for the others to hear. Few seconds later came out Jabber with Dyronn close behind him.

"Man whachu yellin' about?" Jabber asked.

"What's gonnin' on?" No sooner that Dyronn say those words the tower of ice from the waterfall broke free and started falling towards the cottage. Max started turn and help the others get out of the way but from behind he was tackled with the loud growl of the cat. Buried deep in the snow he tried to see past the mount of snow around them. Instead he Rolled over to check her. The cat was grasping her arm with a face clearly showing her pain.

"You okay?" he asked her. She nodded sitting up on her haunches. Getting free of her he stood to find Dyronn and Jabber reaching into the doorway. There they pulled Ragina from the last of the cottage. They all had just narrowly made it free of catastrophe.

"Thank god they made it," Max sighed. Tilting her head the cat had no idea what he had just spoke to. Not aware of her puzzlement in his words he reached over and lifted the cat back to her feet. Her hide had fallen off when she had jumped. Taking the hide from his own back he wrapped it around her. She could only stare at him for the moment. Taking her free arm he led her back to the other three.

"We need to get out of here. We won't make the night with out the house," Max stated only to hear more ice crack from the waterfall. "And it won't be too long before another pillar of ice will come down on us."

"Oh god! Pilla' of ice. This is some David Copperfield stuff. I just wanna go home before we start disapearin' next," Jabber blurted out.

"Shut up Jabber, that isn't gonna help us now," Dryonn ordered before continuing. "So what chu suggest?"

"We should head for the clearing so we can get an idea of where we are at. Then decide what is the best plan of action," Max explained as he started leading the way before any of them could respond. The cat was in tow close behind him.

"Lead tha way," Said Dyronn as he an Jabber carried Ragina over their shoulders. Passing back into the pass between the trees and bushes they were met with all the leaves having frozen solid to their origins if not already fallen to the ground due to dyeing off. The path had become less hidden than any of them had even known. After half an hour of walking they came close to the clearing. Pulling gently on Max's hand he tucked behind a tree truck just as she did.

"What is it?" he asked her.

"It's nothin' Puss is just scared. I'll show you how it's done. Watch this," Jabber said as she just walked out from under the trees.

"Jabber get back here," Dyronn cried in as low of a voice as possible.

"See?! What did I sa..." was all he got out before Jabber was shot in the back with an arrow upon his side. "AH! They got my fat!" he cried falling to the ground. Letting go of the cat's hand Max ran out through a volley of arrows and pulled Jabber back into the safety of the trees. Taking a few close calls while out there, striking his legs and arm. Behind another tree he looked over to the cat that looked back at him. Nodding to each other she peeked around the corner to try and see where the arrows were coming from. Leaning over to do the same Max was hit in the arm. Instantly he felt the burn of something hot from where it ripped his skin open. It must have been pretty sharp to cause that to happen he thought only to watch the skin turn colors and start burning and stinging as the arrow had been tipped with acid.

Going to grab it he drew away his other hand. Zipping across as arrows tried to hit her the cat drew her blade shoving her casted arm against his neck and cut out the meat of his arm that was burning. He screamed out of pain but only gripped the ground beside him as he knew what her actions was doing for him. Once it was cut free she sat back and ducked low. The other two laid silently watching from the shrubs. The cat went to pull her loin from her lower part of her outfit only to be stopped by Max placing his hand on hers.

"No...lets wait," he said. His purpose was to have it cauterized as soon as he had the chance. The trees around them started to creek in an odd and strange way. Looking up at each other the cat and max's hearts just dropped. Those same arrows that had struck max had hit the tree and caused them to give way. In seconds the world had turned upside down as max was hit in the back of the head by the trunk of the tree blacking out. Everything went blurry and the sound in his ears were barely audible. As if that wasn't enough another wave of pressure slammed his body to the ground. Fighting unconscious he glanced up through his blurry eyes to see the cat slashing and fighting off figures in dark shadows before he fell into darkness.

******

Heat held close to his chest and upper body while his legs near froze. Bouncing with the steps of being carried he opened his eyes to see part of the hide blocking his vision. Pain pierced through his left arm where the arrow had hit him. Even with the infected meat removed it still was nearly more than he could bare. Using his hand to lift the hide a bit he was met with the light revealing the cat having carried him on her back like he had her not long ago.

"There is dead cats everywer'. Looks like my dog got loose again. What tha heck happened here?" Jabber asked.

"Elves," Max answered. The cat looked at him over her shoulder and stopped, placing him on the ground. His unsteady legs fought for their footing.

"Elves?! Like, Robbin Hood en' stuff?" Jabber asked.

"No fool! He's talkin' like Lord of the Rings and stuff. Don't you watch movies?" Ragina piped in.

"When you watch Lord of the Rings?" Dyronn puzzled that she would even know.

"What? You think a sista' can't enjoy a white boy? Hell I'd have me some Orlando Bloom," Her words were followed by a bobbing of her head back and forth.

"I ain't even gonna ask what that means" Jabber stated matter of factly. Giving a slight snicker Max shook his head and started following behind the cat on foot the best he could. Reaching out he placed the hide on her back again only to have her stop and take it off herself and cover him again. Clearly she did not need it or she felt he needed it more. Ashes and snow mixed together as far as the eyes could see.

"Ow! What tha?" Jabber said but no one looked back. From under the snow he reached down and dug out the jewelry and accessories the elder cat of the village had worn upon his death. Tucking it in his pockets Jabber looked around to see if anyone was looking. Clearing his throat he caught up with the group without a single mention of his findings.

"How long was I out?" Max asked of the cat. She did not turn but motioned her hand in an arch like the movement of the sun.

"A day?" Max started to panic. She motioned another arch soon after.

"Naw it was like two days dude," Dyronn replied for her. Even though she had answered his question in the first place. Still he needed more time to understand how she communicated he thought. Looking down he pulled his arm out from under the hide to look at how bad the injury had gotten to find it was wrapped. Looking at the cat again he noticed she had pulled the wrap from her leg to cover his wound. There staring back at him was the scar from the whole left by the arrow. That healed a lot faster than he had expected. Yeah it was still pink and looked tender, possibly sore, but her injury on her leg was fast upon the mend. Thinking back he wasn't nearly as surprised. More to the point as to why she slapped his hand for destroying the blade of grass now because he remembered her drinking and chewing it. That has to be the reason for it. Reaching out with his good arm he touched the back of his fingers to her arm. She paused and looked him in the eyes.

"Thank you," he said reaching over and touching his injury.

"Nou goo if nou 'live," she said before going back to her task at hand.

"Aww that's gonna make me sick," Jabber commented only to get hit in the head by Regina.

"Shut tha hell up fool!" she ordered rolling her eyes in annoyance.

"Ma' one day i'm gonna just leave you here with miss meowmix and that redneck. Let you fined for ya own,"

"Jabber you gonna get your ass knocked tha hell out if you say another word," Dyronn warned only to have Jabber mutter under his breath.

"What?" Dyronn questioned.

"Nothin'! I said nothin'," Jabber retorted.

"That's what I thought," Dyronn's words being the last to be uttered out loud. Jabber of course still bantering under his breath and making faces. In the middle of walking the cat reached down and pulled out a log to a more opened area, then another. After making them in an L shape she stared placing rocks in the middle. Max tried to start helping only to have her force him to sit on the log.

"Okay," was all he could say. Once she made a circle with the rocks she stacked wood in the middle. Trying to look around her back that was towards him he found an orange glow grow on the other side. Standing she revealed the fire she made as she tucked away a lighter that was used in the cottage some time ago.

"Girl you smoke? Ah heck yeah," Jabber reached in his pocket and pulled out a broken cigarette. "Come on' light me," he said only to get Dyronn snatched it from across Regina and toss it away.

"Cut that out you fool," he scolded. Not saying a word Jabber only pouted as if he was going to cry. All was completely unseen by Max as he was fighting staring at the cat. More and more she had drawn his attention. He was starting to look forward to seeing her face each and every day. But this was not to be. She had made it clear she was not interested in any of them. The thought of this fact saddened him but it would have to be removed from his mind as fighting the cold was his top priority. Slipping off the log slowly he balled up the best he could inside the hide. Perhaps it could hide the heart break that welled up beneath his breast. Why thought? why was this breaking his heart? She was not human. Heck he was not even sure what she was other than looking like a leopard that could walk up right. All these thoughts just struck him as something odd within his mind he couldn't control. Closing his eyes he just rested his head on his knees and tried not to think about it. All of which was interrupted by the thud of a deer like body hitting the ground next to the fire. He watched her cut up the body and place it on a rock she had put in the fire like he did in her cottage. All of which did not bother him at all until he noticed the deer was like she was in someways. Animal yes, but had the ability to stand up right like any human. That had to be some kind of crime of some sort. Wouldn't it? Sentient beings were always considered something you could not just kill at your own leisure. Then he remembered the age where man had other men as their livestock. A barbaric time indeed. It was no different in that time to kill off those thought to be a lesser being even though they were the same. That must be the rules they live by. This could only mean they would have to be careful how they approached everything in this new world. Looking over at his fellow humans he watched them stand in horror. Seems it disturbed them just as much as it did him. He, like them, wanted to argue and defend the creature, but at that point in time it was more important to survive. Guess he would be the one that would eat the bodies of the other survives if he was stuck with no other way to survive. It's a grim thought. One no one talks about. For now, they were Donner Party, party of five.

Dinner came and went with nothing but entails and bones left. All of them were far more hungry than they thought. So hungry that the convictions of how atrocious the act was now forgotten. Max looked over at the cat who was licking her lips like big cats do. She stared into the fire as did everyone else in an awkward silence. The other three were huddled close to each other. Max reached up and opened up the hide to allow her under. She almost glared at him for a moment.

"Even you can't survive the cold for too long. Besides we can both use the warmth," He reasoned. She paused for a moment then slowly slipped down beside him halfway looking at him the whole way. Once she was down he tried to wrap the hide around them but it was just not covering. After fighting with it he decided it would be easier to just sit one in front of the other. Standing up enough to slip behind her he straddled her over the log. She quickly jumped up on her knees out of caution. Motioning her back down he sat down slipping in front of the log. Again she slowly sat back down placing her rump close but not up against him. Wrapping the hide around them he covered nearly all of both of them. Gradually they were warm and cosy again. Releasing a slight purr, they all looked at her causing her to stop immediately. Knowing the only way they could be completely covered she would have to get closer he used his legs and arms to pull her closer to where his stomach touched her back. Draping Over both their heads and down over their legs he laid his head upon her back and close his eyes. She was soft and cuddly despite the fact she was probably the strongest one there. Her body was detailed in muscles. She still showed those parts that made her distinctly female. Like a way of energy she radiated heat from her body quickly making it so warm under the hide it was impossible to even tell the cold was outside at all.

Exhaustion took over as he melted into the warmth that was him and the cat. Opening his eyes in his dream state he was met with the burn of the sun upon his front and the icy touch of space kissed the edge of his form. Before him was the lit aura of a body before him within a backdrop of space. inside the aura he could see constellations concentrated greatly where the head and chest was. It was the cat! Somehow he was seeing the cat for her inner being from within his own dreams. Staring in awe he watched the various stars twinkle when he picked a single start out of the formations and pinched upon it as if to grab the star. Suddenly he was flooded into blinding light as it presented him with an event that played like a movie and he was the viewer. In the middle was a little cat just like the one with the broken arm. So cute and innocent. A precious sight to see. As it moved along he saw they were next to the waterfalls of her cottage and the old cat that was killed sat next to her as they swung their legs in the water holding sticks with string into the water. Fishing. Surely they were fishing, he thought. From behind a cat that looked a lot like her but older than she was from when he met her wrapped her arms around the tiny cat and the little cat started laughing in the happiest manner. Even in his dream he felt the love that was share with strong emotions only to pause when a sharp thump hit his chest. Another and another until he found himself woken up from his dream.

Standing up the cat had her left side facing him panting heavily. From where she sat steam rose up in plumps around Max. His heart beat wildly as it hit him. That was her soul, a memory from within her own body. But how was this possible? He never had this ability before. Until it struck him. The elf! Whatever the elf did it made his whole body change including abilities. Looking up at her she uttered a string of words in her native tongue, but this time almost as if she was saying a single english word he drew it out understanding it completely.

"Never? Never what?" he asked only able to understand the one word. She did not answer but walked away.

"Did you just meow at her?" Jabber asked. The other three looked at him intently, but he had no answer. Did he really meow back? Or was he speaking her language? Something he would have to figure out later. Standing he thought to follow her only to find she was gone.

"Woah! Ninja cats. Man, this is some freaky stuff gonin' on here," Jabber said not receiving a comment or remark from anyone. Knowing he had to sort it out sooner than later Max looked down and tried to follow the path cut in the snow after her. It only led him so far until a large hole was left and then no more tracks. She took to the trees. While he could climb one tree, he had seen how good these cats could be at moving through the trees. There was no way he would be able to track her down. She was gone until she was ready to be found. For a few more moments he could feel her heart beating as if it was his own, and feel the hurt she was feeling until it just finally melted away. Lowering to his knees he found the overwhelming emotions she had flooded him with coupled with his own crushing him under its weight. Weeping was the only thing that seemed to help him in anyway. Crunching of snow behind him he looked up as the three he left at the fire walked up. Hiding the tears he used positioning the hide to wipe them away unseen.

"Sorry I didn't mean to leave you guys behind," Max excused.

"It ain't no thang man," Dyronn replied.

"We just worried about you guys. What happened to her?" Ragina added.

"Yeah! Did you," Jabber started before leaning in as if to comment to him secretly before continuing, "like touch her somewhere you weren't suppose to?" No sooner those words left his mouth Ragina was wailing away on Jabber. Jabber could only try to duck and cover from the attack. Max thought about the star he touched within her constellation. Considering where it was on the celestial form it might have been. This only adding to his embarrassment.Their only chance to survive in this strange world he made her go away.

"Well what ever you did caused her to wet herself," Jabber added only to be hit again while being lectured. The attack wouldn't last long as another earthquake started. Darting over Max helped Dyronn get Ragina on Dyronn's back and the four of them ran for dear life in the direction they were headed before the cat had disappeared. Before them a section of the snow just vanished causing them to all wobble to a stop over a huge hole before it suddenly changed to a city street and side walk section. All of them falling on their face Jabber instantly started complaining about his arrow injury. Fighting his way free Max stood to dead human bodies littered all over the place killed by trees of the world they were in falling up cars and people alike. Good news was the snow had stopped. Bad news was from all he could tell two worlds were either crashing into each other or one was merging into another. Either way it was bad news for both.

Chapter 5

Parodical

For hours Dyronn and Max spent time checking the bodies for survivors and the cars for supplies. Each time they checked a person Dyronn and Max would give each other a look that spoke volumes as it said 'they didn't make it'. Seemed they would not increase their numbers this time they thought when something met their ears. A cry. It was muffled but near. Both Max and Dyronn scrambled to pry apart a car to get to the back seat. There in a booster seat was a small child no more than toddler age. Somehow he had survived the tree falling upon the car but the driver and passenger had not.

"Got one!" Dyronn said while Max pulled on the bent door of the car as hard as he could to keep it open enough for his partner to pull the kid out. Ragina hopped over taking the child immediately from Dyronn.

"What tha? what are we gonna do with a Chinese baby? huh?" Jabber commented getting hit by Dryonn on the arm.

"Shut up!"

"At this point, I don't think it matters what kind of baby he is. We are out numbered and this helps us just that much more," Max commented as he let go of the door and started pulling out the diaper bag and bottles he could find.

"Help us? How do you figger this half pint gonna help us," questioned Jabbed while Dyronn and Ragina attended to the child.

"If there is a child that made it, there is bound to be another person that made it. Not all the survivors will be toddlers," Max added as he handed the bag to Dyronn. "I'm going to continue looking further."

"Okay Max," Dyronn replied as he helped Ragina move with the child.

"Are you crazy? You're gonna get yourself killed. The elves are fighting the hordes of Mordor. That old bearded white guy is the only one qualified to survive any of this. Are ya listenin' ta me?!" Jabber pleaded.

"Hey Max!" Dyronn called out. Max turned around listening to his words. "Be careful out ther'. This place ain't no joke."

"I hear that,"

"We're gonna move towards those mountains. If we aren't here, we are ther'," he added before Max nodded and started off past the edge of the sidewalk. Stepping down onto the dirt land once more he saw the snow once again. It was thinner than before and clearly melting. The heat had started all of the sudden and without warning. If he was going to find anyone at all it was going to have to be fast. With new determination he took a deep breath and started off in a fair clip.

******

Still dragging the chains that had held him to the wall in the cat village the elf walked up slowly with a smirk upon his face. Standing overlooking a cliff the elf leader admired the blade he had killed the old cat with.

"My lord. How fairs your plans? Is it time?" the elf dragging the chains asked.

"We can proceed if you are eager to achieve our goal," turning back to his fellow elf he waited for a response.

"More than you know. There is a human I need to kill. I bestowed the power of estiral adaption upon him thinking he was an elf. I want it back," snarled the elf. His leader turned the blade handle down over the chained elf's head. Leaning his head back the other elf opened his mouth receiving the drop of blood from the old cat. Instantly he turned into an exact copy of the cat, except in his own clothing and still adorning the chains.

"Exzmer, go with my blessings," the elf leader ordered as he turned back to the falls, and the other elf ran off in a mad laugh that was not his own. "These humans will not be a threat. Our superior might will conquer all," the lord boasted to no one in particular. From behind him an elf ran up fast and dropped to a knee as the leader turned around looking at him.

"We found it lord Vorigus," the knelt elf informed. Vorgius only smiled in a sinister manner.

******

Almost regretting being alone, Max began to wonder how he had done it all those years. Walking and helping random ranchers and farmers for room and board most. Sometimes even working for cash. He had a prepaid phone that he would pay for from different spots as he moved. Reaching into his pocket he pulled out his phone to find the harden glass of the case was shattered in a spiderweb where it had impacted some kind of round object. The cat! He thought to himself. Jabber had that arrow in him and she saw him use it to remove the arrows in her body, she must have used it while he was passed out. Sighing he could just imagine how badly damaged the phone within the case must be. With much more important things to focus on he cleared his thoughts to the task on hand and put his phone back in his pocket. But his mind did not clear. Instead he started to think about the cat and the amazing experience he had that night at the camp fire. What was that? It wasn't normal for sure but he felt everything she did for that short bit of time. It was so euphoric it made him crave it even more. That cat had become his drug of choice, and now he was suffering withdraws. It would be placed on the back burner though as a faint voice called out his direction. Looking around he found nothing that looked like there could have a person calling for him. They kept saying, 'hey you, over here' so they obviously saw him. Looking up he found his answer. In the top of a tree was a woman waving her arms at him. She looked young. Too young. There was no way she could have flew that plane she was clinging on to.

"Stay put! I'm coming up to get you," he said only to hear the branches crack beneath her. Quickly she jumped back in the plane and closed the door. No sooner that she did the limb and plane raced towards the ground. Max could not help stop the plane, but he would be dead if he didn't move. The urge to survive overwhelming his need to help he ran clear of the falling pair. With a loud crash of metal and wood the two hit the ground hard. As soon as everything had stopped moving Max turned back to aid what he was hoping was not a dead girl. As he got closer he saw her head pop out from the windshield. A bit at first and more and more as she squeezed out covered in blood. Reaching in she was pulling on another arm. A man. Jumping up on the plane next to her he saw an older man injured and pinned in the plane.

"Take my daughter and get her out of here. Promise me you will protect her," the man pleaded of max.

"Don't say that dad, don't say that," she cried

"Lets us get you out of here sir. Now can you move your legs?" Max asked only to be interrupted

"No! Get my daughter clear. Promise me!" the man asked again. Behind the plain the fuel had started to burn. Before long the whole forest might be up in flames. He would have to do as the man said. Holding the girl by the arms he fought her impulse to save her father. A strong impulse we would all fight in the same shoes. Simply holding her back was not going to be enough as the flames grew higher. Within the plane the man made not a peep. Max's hunch that he was far greatly injured then originally thought was true. The intensity of the fire had reach such a high level that even the girl's urge to turn away finally kicked in. Not to say she didn't still protest as she conceded. As they were running away from the fire Max realized, he might be cut off from the others. It was a good distance away from them so it's possible the fire won't make it to them, but he might not be able to get back. Sighing he had to let that fall to the back of his mind. There truly was nothing he could do at the moment.

"Why didn't you help him? We could have saved my father if you had only helped," the girls thick southern bell accent rang out.

"Your 'father' knew something we didn't," stopped he turned to face her before continuing, "He just saved your life."

"That's not true! That is not true!!" she yelled ponding on his chest. Grasping his hands he could understand her anger, but could do nothing to quell it.

"Look, I am sorry about your dad, but the fact is at how fast that fire lit up the fuel would not have given us enough time to unpin him from the wreckage. Your father knew that and ordered us away because of it. Just know that he died...so you could live," what was he saying? Of all the times to give words of wisdom was this really the right time? Turning away he continued walking when he remembered he dropped the pack. Instead of pausing he kept going. That pack was far too close to the fire and heading back for that might make the situation worse. The leaves behind him rustled with the girl catching up to him.

"I'm sorry. You are right. But that was my father. I would have rather died then let him die like that," she argued.

"And you would have damned his soul in his eyes,"

"What did you say?" she was shocked to hear him say such words. Turning he looked her in the eyes.

"Your dad's whole existence was to raise and protect his daughter...you. Now put yourself in his shoes. As a parent would you let your child died because they are trying to protect you?" Continuing on he left the girl with something to think about. Didn't take long for her to realize his words were true as she jogged to catch up to him and walked by his side.

"My name is Annabelle. Everyone calls me Annie," she said softly.

"Max," He said as the both of them fell into silence. Wondering around the rest of the day, they came across cars, trucks, and vans. None of them having what he was looking for, and even less to Annie. She still wasn't sure what he was doing in the first place. Finally he saw a cargo van. Thinking it was going to be another lost cause he passed it by.

"Your just goin' to pass it by? You've checked every car from here to kingdom come," she pointed out.

"Fine," he said turning back around and opening up the back door of the van. It had tubs full of food and other supplies. Closing the door he took another look. It was a dooms day cult's van that he faintly remembered from the news some time back. This was either good luck or bad luck. Some of the tubs were opened and some of the food packages had been opened. Looking around the van and into the surrounding area. They had to be there somewhere. But did he want to wait and get these people to join them? If what he had heard from the news was true the answer would be an irrefutable no. So he will have to go with his second thought. Steal it.

"Wow there is a lot of food in here," she said stepping into the van.

"Yep, and we're going to take it. Head to the front i'm going to shut the doors and we can get out of here," he explain.

"Okay," she said stepping over the tubs and getting in the passenger seat. Max closed the doors quickly and went to the drivers side at a good clip. He didn't wanted to get caught by this cult if they were still around. Jumping in the drivers seat he found a little blood on the steering wheel and shifter. Looking around they both found some more on the dash. Looking at each other they agreed it was time to go. Shutting the doors they both clicked on their belts and Max started the van throwing it in gear and pealing out. Probably not the best idea, but panic can cause you do things you wouldn't normally. All he wanted to do was get as far away from there as fast as possible. Most of his stay in this unknown land has been hostile and even life threatening. The last thing he was willing to do was chance getting hurt. Of course that was what was really on his mind. It was the cat with the broken arm. In fact she consumed most of this thoughts that he couldn't hear his passenger warn him about the tree. Catching himself at the last moment he almost slammed into it head long only to turn at the last moment. Heart pounding he pulled over putting the van in park. Looking over his shoulder behind them at the tree that almost ended them he sighed.

"What's wrong with you? You almost got us killed," his passenger pointed out. The truth was he knew it. The cat had distracted him and she wasn't even there.

"I need to rest. We can get started again tomorrow," he explained as he exited. Without even putting a second thought to it Max began to build a fire spot exactly like the cat had. It was only when he was looking for a lighter that he even realized he had done it. From over his shoulder the girl passed him a metal lighter.

"Here. I want it back though," she explained finding her a spot on the log. Looking at her he could see the fight she was still having about the loss of her dad. A feeling he knew in a different manner. It was not the time to think about such things he thought as he lit the fire feeding it until it was strong on its own. Not sitting near the log he found his spot next to the fire where every licking flame looked so close to the cats colors that he found himself lost in them. If there was a way to have been bewitched it must be from the cat, he thought. She was the one that kept close to him since she had come across him. Though she didn't seem to have that kind of power. But here he was non-stop thinking about her as if she was the love of his life or an instant crush. It was true this didn't really pick up until they had that one night. It was not intimate like one would think of but it was something so personal there were no words to explain how it felt in his mind.

Suddenly his attention was drawn away as a sound of a cracking stick met his ears. Wiping around his heart nearly leapt out of his his chest with joy at the sit of the cat. He started towards her only to have her move a foot back as if she was going to leave. Thinking better of it he stood his ground and just stared as he fought back tears.

"Oh my god! We need to run or that things going to kill us," the young girl whispered.

"No she won't. I've know her better than that," he said waiting for the cat to make a comment, but she never did. Seems that connection they had affected her as well. From the looks of it not in the same way as far as he could see.

"You know that thing?"

"She is not a thing," he said as he turned her direction before continuing, "she's...more."

"I think you're crazier then a betsy bug," the young girl said in her souther bell. Max and the cat continued to stare at each other almost as if they were waiting for the other to react.

"Nou way lon' you find new?" the cat asked. While her words were as broken as ever it didn't take a rocket scientist to tell she was showing signs of green.

"She was stuck in a tree. Even lost her father. What was I suppose to do?" Max's words made a point as she lowered her head blinking a few times. She had caught herself back in the loop of emotions again. Composing herself again she took a step forward.

"You..." the cat tried to begin only to have to start over. "Ow you tuch...?" she asked tapping the center of her chest.

"Your soul?" Max pipped in. The cat nodded.

"What are you talkin' about? You touched what?" the young girl pipped in. Max started to reply but instead decided it would be best to say nothing at all.

"I am not sure how I was able to touch your soul. All I know is I...felt...It felt like nothing else I have ever experienced before," Max took a step forward. The cat watched his foot intently. Looking back up at him she took another step herself. Tapping her head she continued.

"You many," the cat explained.

"Yeah, me too," Max sighed in return.

"Somethings wrong with you Max,"

"Annebelle please hush," looking back Max scorned as the child sat down. Turning back around he watched the swaying tail as the cat walked away. "Yeah...mood killer," Max muttered to himself before sitting back down himself. Max hardly slept that night. All he could think of was the cat and how he was so close yet so far away. The increasing heat didn't help.

"Why is it so damn hot?" Annebelle complained as she sat up unbuttoning her flannel shirt.

"Wow, you talk like that normally?" Max asked of the girl.

"Sorry, but it's really hot and I can't stand being hot," she explained as she tossed the shirt behind her laying her head back down. It would have made Max more uncomfortable if she was not wearing the tank top. Really what was making him uncomfortable was the fact this young girl was left in his charge and he had no idea what he was going to do. Looking over to the horizon just above the mountain line he could see lights first rays. Standing up he tapped the girls boots on the heel.

"We need to get moving," Max ordered as he headed for the van. The girl sat up almost angrily.

"Fine, but I'm driving," she claimed.

"You have a license?" Max asked turning back to her.

"I have a permit. But I know how to drive," She exclaimed. Grabbing the door before she could open it Max looked her in the face.

"Yeah and I know how to rob a bank, but doesn't mean I should," Max argued.

"Seriously? God!" she cried as she stormed around the van. Max shook his head as he got into the van. What to do with her indeed. He never had to deal with kids as he never had any of his own. In fact he avoided relationships all together to the extent when a girl or woman acted as if they liked him he would move on to the next town. Technically there were no towns like the since in which he was thinking in this world, and if he did he would leave a girl to fend for herself that was too young to survive from what he could see. Hardened by farm life himself, he could tell she had seen hard labor before. But this was different. This was a matter of life or death on a whole other level.

Sitting in the seat of the van he turned the key to find the van struggle a bit before it finally started. Just happy it was still working he let it pass as he put the van in gear. Driving away he found room to turn around and headed back for Dyronn and his group. They would need the food in the back of the van as much as he would.

"Wait, why are we going back? I thought you said..." the girl started only to be interrupted.

"We have to pick up the rest of my group. They are not going to last long with that baby in hand," he explained.

"Okay, then let's hurry up. The quicker we can get out of here the better," she almost pouted. There was something else he had remembered he didn't like about kids. It didn't take long for Max to back track all the way to where he had picked up the girl. Smoke and embers scattered for more than the length of a football field. Glancing over he watched the girl as she started to get emotional at the sight of the remains of the plane.

"There was nothing we could do for him. He was pinned in and we would not have gotten him out in time," Max pipped in.

"Yeah," but that was not what she thought. Her honest opinion was Max let her father die. The shock must have been too fresh because she had not even started grieving as of yet, Max thought to himself. Keeping on moving he was almost back to where he had left his group to find no sign of them. Placing the van in park he looked around. The girl did the same. She was not nearly as focused as he was. Suddenly the van began to shake from the girl trying to lock the door and look in the glove box for something. Whipping around Max was met with Jabber knocking on the window in the most comedic way.

"That guy is so crazy sometimes," Max said as he opened his door.

"What tha hell are you doin'? They're going to rape me and kill you," she commented. Reaching in to the van he grabbed the keys.

"That is the other part of my group. And they are not going to rape and kill anyone," Max explained closing the door to the van. Great we have a raciest other then Jabber, he thought to himself. How exactly was that going to work? He was not going to leave Jabber and the others just because he had promised to take care of this girl. She will have to just learn to deal with her feelings about them and move on. It was the only option she had if she was going to survive. In greetings Dyronn and Max shook hands while Ragina placed her hand on his shoulder. Looking down at the toddler he watched the little boy cling to Ragina's neck.

"It's good ta see ya again brotha," Dyronn said with a smile.

"Yes we are glad to have you back," Ragina added.

"Well I did say I was going to find anyone that needed help and see if I could find some supplies. That van is full of food in the back," Max told them.

"Serious?" Dyronn questioned only to get a smile and a nod form Max. Jabber meanwhile danced around them like some kind of idiot about Max returning with a van and more white people. Something that would probably be more trouble then he really wanted to deal with considering he already had one person in the van that had a problem and of course the return of the other. Looking over his shoulder at the girl he watched her make obscene gestures at Jabber. Jabber of course doing them right back.

"And it seems that my passenger and Jabber have a common hatred in common," Max said to his chagrin.

"Damn. That's not what we need right now. I can keep Jabber In check. I'll let choo deal with that one," Dyronn said pointing to the girl in the van that continued her gestures with Jabber. Neither of them being more mature then the other.

"Yeah. We're going to have to," Max said much to his own chagrin. "Anyways how about you guys pile in and we can get moving. Turning to cut between Jabber and Annebelle Max tried to unlock the door with his keys only to find the girl holding the lock down.

"Unlock the door," he demanded. All he could see was her face and lips in the motion of defiance. He tried a few more times then figured it wasn't worth it.

"I'll just have to unlock the back door. Come on you can get in the back for now. Once I can get her out of the seat we can have Ragina sit there," Max said heading to the back of the van.

Opening the door he watched them all get in, when it struck him. Ragina was walking on her own.

"Where..." Max started.

"That kitty we met came back and gav' it to me," Ragina explained.

"Yeah man, she even helped her put it on," Dyronn added. Max's eye brows lifted. She came back to help the group. Seems she had not gone far after all.

"Yeah your pussy came back...Ha! get it. Pussy? Y'know like puss in boots? Sep she has no boots," Jabber tried his wit only to find himself being told to shut up once again and pulled into the van. Shutting the door Max fought to keep his focus on the task at hand again. The cat was as good of a person as he had thought.

Chapter 6

Waterfalls

Driving most of the day the group dealt with the arguments between Jabber and Annebelle. Not to mention the racial tensions the two were causing throughout the day. Tired, hungry and just over all wanting to have a break from the whole thing Max pulled over when he spotted a river with a small cascading falls. Was not as glorious as the ones the cat had at her cottage, but they would do. Stepping out the van Max heard nothing of the fights of words behind him nor any other problem as he set up a fire just out of sight of the falls on the other side of the van. One by one the arguing parties joined him around the fire as it got late. What was it all over? He really didn't care. Only the cat was on his mind since he was told about the prosthetic leg made of wood and leather the cat had made. That night he half expected to see the cat show up again, but she didn't. The next morning he woke first before the sun had lit the world enough to see clearly. Being he was up first he thought he could go and take a dip in the water before everyone else could wake up. Getting near the falls he rubbed his drowsy eyes. The lack of sleep kept him unaware and that bothered him. Splashing the water would help with not only the heat but also wake him up he figured. Stripping down to nothing next to the falls he turned around to find the cat staring right back at him with water running down her body. both of them went wide eyed. Neither of them had even noticed the presence of the other due to how focused they were on each other. She reached up to touch his face as they were lost in each other's eyes. He lifted his hand brushing the back of it along her body until he too was touching her face. She blinked her eyes slowly as she began to purr. Leaning in his lips aimed to meet with hers. Her purr went away. Instead they met again in the dark space looking upon the form he had seen once before only in his dreams. That was her. The radiating form was her body bared to him in its purest form. But this time the form was looking right back at him. Facing eye to eye. The kiss of the cold from space was less than before. He could not help but to explore her body as it was only to notice something he had missed before. Deep in the arm back and leg were stars of a different color. The arm and back were dark blood red in glow and the leg lighter so. He reached out and this time took hold of the red star. It burned hotter than anything he had felt before. Soon it extinguished and was turning normal again. A rush of darken visions fluid his mind. They were hers. Her hate and anger. All of it was aimed at the elves. It showed him a much older elf, one he had not see before. Friends with the older cat of her village there were other creatures of all kinds around. Deer, sheep, antelope, even hyenas walking around her village as if it was some kind of market. Letting go of the star he looked down at his finger tips to see a reddish black glow emanate from them. It was no wonder she was showing red in those stars. They seem to hold her more aggressive thoughts in them and the memories that accompany the target of her thoughts. Letting go once the start was out he looked back at her to noticed her glowing aura grew. Going for the red stars he one by one snuffed them out over and over causing his pain in his fingers to increase and spread to his hand. Halfway through the red stars in her arm a force was gripping hard and pushing his arm away. No! Not now, he thought. He had to know what was so important about that older elf. Why was he so important? Just as quick as their experience had started he was found stumbling back a bit back in reality. His legs wobbled as well as his body. She was visibly shaken to. Both had the look as if the greatest connection two souls could happen just happened to them.

"Oh my god! NO! I can't unsee dat. Where is the fire. I need-I need to burn out my eyes," came the voice of Jabber as he scurried off still ranting and raving. Turning slowly Max's quivered to find the young girl as she stepped backwards wide eyed before dashing off.

"That...No en' well," the cat said out loud.

"I have a feeling we are going to catch hell for that one Garliva," his words had not even finished as he turned to her eye to eye again. Each time they had connected she learned more and he learned more. In fact his arm hurt right where she had been shot. A spot on his back and upper thigh too. It was a mental link. A melding of souls. Those were not stars, they were memories. Elves were the target of her hatred and they shot her arm which made sense that those stars involving them would attach to where they shot her. More importantly each of them helped him understand how her mind worked at the same time meaning they could understand each other more and more. Smiling he looked down at his fingers to find the tips bleeding and his fingers and hand swollen. Seems there was another part of it. The injury transferred to a new target when those stars were extinguished. His hand. Looking at her he noticed she had been covering her more private areas when the other two were there but uncovering them as she stared back at him. This was wrong. How could it be he was falling for this cat before him? There was nothing logical at all about it. When the thought struck him. What that elf did in the village! It must have warped his mind and caused this vile deviation. Focusing back on her he could not fight the feeling and just let go as she pet his face.

"You soul...es beautiful," she said as she leaned in cupping his face in her soft and gentle paws. The softest purr he had ever heard from her started as she extended her lips in the fashion one would as she kissed him. For a cat that didn't understand it when he did it to her the first time she picked up passionate kissing very quickly. Or was that his knowledge she was working off of. She was speaking his language better than ever before and her mannerisms were becoming more and more human. This time however they didn't fall into each other on a celestial level. More her controlling the situation than before, or perhaps it needed for them to place body to body for it to work. Placing his hands on her hips he smiled back only to have her notice something odd about him. Looking down she saw his hand and that it was bleeding. Quickly she pulled away and tossed him his pants as she threw on her own clothing. Just enough time to get his last leg in his pants he struggled to get them buttoned up only to have her drag him barefoot to the group who was arguing at the fire. The girl was in the van with doors locked.

"Wher' is bondages?" Garliva demanded more then asked.

"What tha' shit! When did chu learn to talk?" Jabber said stopping his fussing.

"Bondages!" she ordered again.

"I-I think they are in the back of the van," Turning directions Max was shocked as she knew what a van was as she dragged him right to it. Trying to pull the handle she turned to him as he pulled the keys with his bloody fingers from his pants and passed them to her. She looked up on the key and the blood that was dripping off of them. Unlocking the van she quickly threw open the door as the young girl yelled at her for doing so. Grabbing the kit she pulled the bandages and turned to max to find he had falling over vomiting violently. Growing dizzy Max looked up at her as he was half hunched over before falling to the ground and passing out. Dropping to her knees she attended his hand before she snatched him up into her bosom weeping and rocking. He had fallen ill from the poison her village had. Now she would loose another. Just then an earthquake began. The cat's cries could hardly be heard over the sound of the earth fighting back against what ever unnatural force was ripping it apart. Only this time Garliva and Max were right in the way as they were whisked away with the section of ground as it fell. Landing hard she fell over Max. Scrabbling she still sobbed but checked the man who was out cold. Not sure where they were she scooped him up and moved him into a large barn that was only a few yards away. Darting through the door she tossed max on a pile of hay and turned back to close the doors. Then backed away and turned to max once more. All the doors and shutters on the rickety old barn rattled. A storm was coming. A rather large one at that, sensed the cat. She stayed close to the ground hovering over Max protecting him with her life. Looking down at him she wanted badly to take it all away. When the thought struck her. Maybe she could. Every time they were close to each other they would go into that strange place where they could see stars inside each other's bodies. If nothing else it was worth a try. Wrapping her arms around him she pressed his body to hers. Nothing happened.

"Nou. You hav' to com' back tu me," she said as she released enough to look him in the face before drawing him close again. Still not a thing happened. Tears started to develop in the corners of her eyes. She never had the chance to save her brother. She has lost her niece and even betrayed by her grandfather. This strange looking creature in her hands was all she had left to attach to, and have become closer to him than anything or anyone else in existence. And she was going to loose him as well. Just then she remembered that it was skin contact that caused them to connect before. In fact at the water falls she was not wearing a thing. Standing up she stripped down and tossed it to her side as she knelt back down with only the splint he had put on her remaining. Leaning over she hugged him to her tight. She could feel his labored breathing. Even the warmth of his chest but there was no connection made. Apparently he had to be concuss for it to work. With no more thoughts or ideas she started to cry uncontrollably. Only thing to bring her out of it was the creaking of the barn door as it swung open. From the flood of light came the end of a shotgun with a farmer in overalls. He turned her way in complete shock. All the farmer could see was a large zoo animal had escaped and the blood all over max from the tips of his fingers didn't help.

"Joey go call the police. Tell them theres a lion or something here eating a man," it was no wonder he thought such a thing as she was growling at the man as soon as she could see him. Noticing he wasn't an elf she changed her tune.

"Wait! Nou goo. He urt. Ples elp em," She pleaded. For a second time the man was shocked. Lowering his gun he asked inquisitively.

"What did you say?"

"H...urt. He nee...elp," she said trying to slow down to speak clearly, "Ples." Placing his gun agains the wall he understood her enough to know she was no threat. Walking over he saw she was no normal cat. She was probably one of those furries the people on the news talked about. Crouching down he saw the blood was from Max's fingers and not his body. Not that it was much better but at least the man wasn't dead in his barn.

"We need to get him to a doctor," the farmer said as he turned his head to the sound of sirens in the distance speeding their way. Being a small town the police were usually board and always ready for some excitement. Meaning dealing with a large lion was going to be the most excitement they would have for a long time and they were not going to pass it up.

"But you need to get out of here. They will shoot you on site," the farmer explained only to get a tilted head from her. "They will kill you. now go! hide somewhere." Heeding his warning she started climbing post nearest him with her claws. The farmer watched her go up the pole thinking to himself that was the oddest thing he had ever seen.

"That is not a normal cat," muttered the farmer. Looking back at max something green next to him caught the farmers attention. Reaching over he lifted up Garliva's garments.

"What in tha?" was all he could really say. From behind him the police came in the barn door over to the farmer looking down at Max. The police did not notice the clothing in the farmers hands but instead knelt down to help out max when they noticed the claw marks going up the post. Looking up they saw her eyes staring back at them. Without warning they started firing their pistols at the eyes. As soon as they had seem them the eyes were gone. In a flurry of shuffling around the police ushered the farmer out and two others carried out Max on their shoulders. The last one out closed the barn door. As far as they knew they had the creature pinned and there was no way it could get out. What they didn't know was the other end of the barn was open. Garliva decided that staying there at that moment would surely be the end of her so she jumped down on the field of corn and started running as low as she could. Apparently it wasn't low enough because one of the officers saw her and started firing his gun at her. Needing even lower she started moving on all fours as fast as she could go. Which did not help matters. Now they were sure it was a big cat they were shooting at. Max on the other hand was being attended to until an ambulance showed up and carried him off to a hospital.

******

The chase had gone on for hours into the night. Her eyes were greatly adapted to these conditions but now it was not only police but zoo and safari experts trying to help capture her now. There had been a few close calls and they had almost cornered her numerous times. Thankfully she was able to get away before they could even close the trap shut. Taking a breather she leaned up against a tree closing her eyes for the moment breathing in deep. Looking down at her hands she could see the blood on her body from Max still lingering. When it finally came to her attention. The splint had broken. The wooden spoon was gone and the stick in two pieces. Her arm didn't hurt as bad anymore. Max had taken it away. Each of the stars he touched moved it to his hand and that was why his hands were hurt. Being that they were near a poisoned waterfall it got in his blood and now he was sick just like her fellow villagers. Gripping her hands in anger she gritted her teeth flattening her ears to her head growling loudly. Big mistake. She had forgotten she was hiding from the others of

Max's kind. Turning from the lights that were swinging around in the dark she was hit with several bites on her side and tail. Jumping into action she ran as fast as she could until she was suddenly struck with uncontrollable sleep and fell over on her face rolling in the dirt. Coming to a stop some men in white lab coats came up behind a small military group in camouflage uniforms.

"Well seems we have another one. And this one isn't in the public eye," one said out loud. The lights were getting closer.

"We need to move. If they find us here there would be a huge mess to clean up,"

"Agreed. Let's get back to base 51. Bring her along quickly. Leave no trace of us being here," another said as they all disappeared into the night.

Chapter 7

Apart

Several days had passed before Max finally woke up. The first thing to greet his sight when he woke was the nurse checking the drip.

"Oh good you're awake. I'll go get the doctor," she said leaving the room. Sitting up in his bed he looked around. How did he get here? Last thing he could remember was sharing time with the cat that called herself Garliva. Called herself, not actually. It was what her name was according to what was told to him from a vision. Or was it a dream.

"Good morning sir. How are we today?" the doctor asked speaking as soon as he hit the door. The nurse followed close behind him.

"Where am I?"

"You are on the forth floor of First General Medical Center," The doctor replied.

"How,..." he started to ask only to be interrupted.

"How did you get here? Your employer. I think his name was McNealson. A farmer not far from here. He remembered you...uh, Jimmy was it? Or was it James?," the doctor wondered as he clicked his pin ready to write.

"I uh,"

"Well if you can't remember it's okay, we can come back to that later. So how do you feel currently?"

"I'm confused, where is Garliva?"

"I'm sorry I am not familiar with a...Garliva. Please breath deep," the doctor had placed the stethoscope agains his back. "Again," he ordered. "And Again," once completed he took them off and placed them around his neck jotting a few things down. The nurse was folding a few things in the corner and restocking supplies in the room. Leaning back down he could only stare at the ceiling.

"Welp you seem to be in good health. In a few hours we can release you. Next time be sure not to just drink from any water source. Because next time you might not get so lucky," The doctor warned as both him and the nurse left the room. Left with his thoughts he tried to find some way to verify that it wasn't a dream he had experience, but thought of nothing. Taking a deep breath, perhaps he could write it all down It would be the makings of a good book, he thought to himself as he placed his hand upon his forehead. The sudden surreal feeling covered him as his eyes widened. His fingers were wrapped all the way to the middle of his arm. It was real. Then she was out there. Possibly in his world. Oh no! Humans throughout history have destroyed anything that was too scary for them to handle, and Garliva was a big cat with the ability to reason like a human. Panic would quickly ensue.

Jumping from the bed he found he was without clothing. Great, I will have to get my clothing back, he thought as he opened the door and started down the hall but thought twice as he saw several men in business suits and uniformed officers. He was going to try and just pass them or continue on his way, but they pointed at him and told him to stop. This was not good. As quick as a rabbit spotting a fox he darted the other way through the people in the hall. It only took him moments to get to the elevator. Inside he pressed the buttons on the wall. If they had no idea which floor he was getting off on maybe he would have an easier chance of getting out. Jumping off the elevator on the first floor it stopped he moved over to the next elevator to find it was in use. Have to use the stairs, he thought. Dashing down the stairs he noticed there were other footsteps meeting each step. Pausing, they were right below him trying to head him off. That was problematic.

He would have to think of something else when it struck him. He could put on scrubs and a mask it would be harder to identify him. Going out the nearest door he started searching everywhere he could until he finally found the supply area of the floor. Grabbing a few at random he threw them on and then grabbed a face mask off the wall. Now he was ready. Walking with a calm and cool attitude he headed for the bottom floor. As he passed the lobby he noticed the image on the TV showed some more animals like Garliva. Taking a step back he looked closer. They were the ones that were in her village. In fact it seemed they had showed up where the barber shop had disappeared from. To add to it they were cured and being kept in a concentration camp for observation. This would be good news to tell Garliva as soon as he found her, but he had to get back on track. Turning to the front doors again he walked right out them. Looking back he finally realized his mistake. Those were just normal scrubs, they were operating scrubs and only the doctors wore them. Which means he wasn't a discreet as he thought he was. Ripping the mask away his bare feet slapped the ground with each movement forward as he went into a full on sprint.

******

Day in, day out since she had been captured she had been strapped to a bed that was tilted upright. Poked and prodded she had lost enough blood from whatever they were doing to want to black out. She had not eaten, nor drank anything in days and it was taking its toll. Perhaps it was time to just let go, she thought. Even with that thought one thing kept her going. Max. Of course she knew it was not his real name, but the very thought of him kept her moving. Almost as if his soul actual pushed her on to survive. When in fact it actually did even if they did not know it. Her fur was matted to her skin from sweat. Something she had not been able to do previously. Usually she would pant until cooled down, but the combination was working better than before. This wasn't going to matter long unless she was allow to eat and drink. Looking around the thought that these people were nothing like Max. They were cruel and mean and not far off from being elves. Walking up to her a man a suit with a United States flag pin on the left collar cupped his hands behind his back as he looked on in awe.

"What have you learned about this creature?" he asked.

"Well sir we found that she is not like anything we've seen before," one of the scientists explained. Not that it was needed to be said as the man in the suit gave him a disapproving look.

"Sorry sir, what I mean is she is not human, and not really animal. She has the genetic markers in her from a leopard, but there is no human markers at all. She is as if she had evolved from the four legged beast into," he paused to motion both hands at Garliva, "this."

"So are you saying cats are evolving?" the man in the suit asked.

"Oh not at all, this cat is not from our world. A whole new species," the scientist explained.

"Just like the others found in New York. Thankfully we were able to sneak this one out of the public eye before the media could interferer," Tilting his head the man looked at her chest before pointing at it, "Is that..."

"A breast yes," the scientist answered before the man could finish his words. Turning back the man raised an eye brow before he started to walk out.

"You should probably look into getting a girlfriend," said the man before disappearing beyond the doors. Looking the scientist was puzzled as she had been brought in her current condition.

"Get a girlfriend? I haven't time for that my work is too important," he said snapping his fingers motioning over a few men who uncuffed her from the bed and dragged her off to a glass box with air holes around the sides. The glass was easily four or more inches thick. Dropping her on metal floor with a thunk the two men walked out. Placing a plate of food on the floor beside her the lead scientist watched her for a moment try to lift herself up off the floor. Catching himself he placed a second bowl on the floor next to the food and poured a bottle of water into it before leaving her to her own devices. She looked at the food, raw meat, and almost cringed. Why? She thought. Was it not the food she would eat back home before she met Max. Max! That is right. He had shown her how to make the food tastier. Where was he now? She wondered as her arms shook. Which was a thought she would have to revisit later. If she didn't eat she wouldn't live long enough to see him again. Grabbing the meat with one hand she placed it in her teeth and worked at ripping it free so she could chew her bite.

"See! I knew she would be like our big cats. She eats raw meat," the scientist uttered in a bit of revelry. Jotting down notes with his digital pin on his tablet he noted every detail he could. So it was true, she was nothing more then some toy for them to study and experiment on until they were bored, she thought. What she didn't know was the man in the suit that left was not interested in studying her but more the quickest way to kill her kind. For now she would have to play along. She needed time to rebuild her strength. Lifting the bowl of water she cupped her lips around the rip and drank from its contents. This shocked the scientist almost immediately as he pressed against the glass. Reaching in his pocket for a cellphone the scientist made a call.

"You have got to see this!" he said as he pointed the phones camera at her.

******

Max had finally out ran his pursuers. This had not come soon enough as his feet were bleeding from the harsh travel on the concrete. Not that it was something on his mind as he felt Garliva, and he knew she was in real trouble. But how was he going to find her? he wasn't even awake when he was taken to the hospital. Then right in front of him an old beat up pick-up pulled in front of him.

"Johnny! What are you doing out here boy?" the old man said. It was the old man from the barn. Not that he knew that.

"Do I know you?" he asked.

"Yeah your uh, cat person, and you were in my barn remember?" the old man started when he thought about it and it was curious. "Why are you wearing those hospital clothes? Don't the doctors wear those?"

"They do. Where did the cat go?" Max asked as he walked around to the passenger side of the truck.

"Oh I have no idea son, but she went running off in my field. Not likely you'll find her now."

"Take me there. I have to find her she is in grave danger," Max explained slamming the door shut.

"Okay," the old man said as he hopped in the truck as well and the two were off. They were several hours outside of town before they finally stopped. Their conversations were brief enough to learn that Max had at one time worked for the farmer in his travels. Apparently he was a good worker because the farmer regretted seeing him go. Which was also why the farmer was visiting him as often as he could to see if he could help him.

Pulling into the field they didn't go far before he saw parts of the L shape wood he had bonded her arm with laying on the ground broken. It had finally worked its way free. But that really wasn't what caught his attention. The fact there were usually tracks from trucks and a set of business like shoe prints in the ground made him think. It was a lot worse than he had thought. Exhaling a deep breath it crossed his mind. He was still in medical scrubs and bare foot. There was no way he would be able to track down that car. He stood back up and just stared off in the distance the tracks led.

"I'm sorry to impose but I need a few things," he turn back to the farmer, "I need a change of clothes and if possibles some shoes."

"Come on. We can head back to the house. I'll get you what you need," the old man replied already heading to his truck. Opening the passenger door Max noticed Garliva's clothing. A spark hit him, she was in more trouble than he thought. Without her clothing she did indeed have a human like body. But only if you saw it at the right angle. Otherwise it looked just like a leopard and she could easily be mistaken for just another large cat. Reaching down he took hold of the clothing.

"No...she is," he paused before looking back up to the farmer. "I've lost her," looking down at the clothing he continued, "Possibly forever."

"Listen son. I've lived a long time. I've seen a lot of things, but I have never seen anything like her before in my life. Now I know she is a tough girl. And while I don't understand whatever it is you have with her...I'm sure she is still alive. Somewhere," the old man said as he pulled out of the field and back to his home. Once at his home Max followed him in and stood in the front foyer. It wasn't long before the old man brought down some boots in a box that was unopened, and some clothing that was clearly too large for him. Looking at the coveralls first he helped them out to see that were the farmers. A few inches too short and far too wide. It would have to do. Draping them over his arm he looked in the box. A pair of boots lay before him unused still with the laces in the bottom eyelet and tucked neatly inside the footwear. Taking the box he smiled to the farmer as the farmer handed him a shirt far too small for the farmer.

"Here you go son. Over the years we have collected various clothing and such that just never did fit. Being we are so far from the city we didn't bother to take them back. Should have...Just never did," said the farmer as a door could be heard creaking around the corner.

"Hareld is that you? Who...," the old lady paused for a moment before rushing up and hugging Max. "It's good to see you again Johnny."

"Ma'am same here," Max said out of respect.

"Go ahead and get dressed. Then you can eat supper with us. We can discuss your next move." the farmer said as max went to the door the man was pointing at. As he went by the stairs he heard another voice and a young boy coming down the stair casing. Ignoring it for the moment he went into the bathroom. It was a small bathroom, barely enough room for the toilet that was in it. Most of the clothing went on smooth and easy. Only the boots took time as he had to lace them up. Getting dress wasn't really what was on his mind. It was the cat. She needed him, or at least that was the feeling he got. As he stepped out of the bathroom he brushed down the coveralls with his hands trying to get back that extra few inches that the farmer was missing in height.

"Oh good you're finished. Come on in here," he directed of Max. Following the old man he turned the corner where the other two were waiting for him and the old man to return. Food was laid out across the elongated table with a spread of all things the farmer and his wife grew. The smell was intoxicating. His stomach growled and his mouth watered just to the smell alone. Sitting down he partook of the food with the farmer and his family. Recalling stories of when he had been passing through and helped an old man. Seemed the farmer had never forgotten it, and for good reason. He had been changing a tire under his tractor along the road and the jack had given way. Max pulled him out from under the falling tractor before it crushed him. It was such a memory that it was clear the old man felt it was a debt that could never be repaid. Even if that was not how Max saw it. As for the young man that sat at the table with them, that was the old man's grandson that was visiting for the summer. Basically a summer job for the young man to earn some money to play with once he got back home.

The evening events finally wrapped up and everyone went to bed. Max was given a spare bedroom for the night. The same room he was offered his first stay. Laying there eyes opened he tried to find every way that Garliva's capture was his fault from her protecting him to trying to draw off trouble. The list seemed to never end until he finally fell asleep. Even there he found no relief as he could see her pinned to a table that was held vertical. Her body uncovered and withered away. Her ribs showed from lack of food and water. Body showed signs of the constant drawing of blood. He watched as scientists walked in and did varies things almost as if stop-capture motion pictures. she hardly even moved. As his focus brought him closer to her he noticed a man in a suit, hands clasped behind his back start to align with her movement, stop before her. She looked right at Max, 'elp me' she muttered as the man looked over his shoulder right at him.

"You'll never help her in time," he stated right at Max. Sitting straight up in bed he knew she was in trouble. Jumping from the bed he quickly dawned his clothing and boots and ran downstairs waking up the farmer. It was still pitch outside.

"Johnny? Where's the fire?" the farmer asked. Max stopped mid step.

"I know where they have her. She needs me. They are killing her Herald," Max pleaded. Going serious the farmer looked him in the eyes.

"Let me grab my jacket."

Chapter 8

Savior

"She'll be hell to keep running, don't idle too low. Also second gear likes to stick. Remember none of the gauges work and only half the lights work," The old man said as he got out from under the truck on his creeper. Walking over to the work station he pulled the grease rag from his pocket and wiped off his hands then tossed it down.

"Are you sure about this? I have no idea if I will ever be able to return. These guys mean business," Max explained.

"Son, I've seen that look before. It was just before my father went into the second world war. There was no changing his mind no matter what any one said. And we both know you are there right now. For all you have done for me this is the least I can do for you. Now let me get all the headlights and tail lights running and you are good to go," the farmer said as he picked up a few boxes he had stacked against the wall. The whole time he thought about how his own father had read the newspapers and grew more and more angry. Now because of the injustice that the Nazi's had brought to the Jews, not even to all of Europe. No, it was the fact that they threatened his own family simply by getting too close to America. If only. True the Nazi's were going to target United States sooner or later, but the truth was the American publicity and propaganda was really far more aggressive than things really was. Tossing max the keys from his jacket pocket he smiled to the young man. Max started to thank him only to have the old man raise his hand.

"Don't. Just promise me you will do right by that cat friend of yours and come back to see me afterwards," the farmer requested. Max nodded then reached in and hugged him. The gratitude was very apparent.

Determination on his face Max tossed Garliva's clothing into the seat then sat down in the truck and closed the door. The farmer walked to the door where the window was down. Max reached down for the choke only to be stopped.

"Don't touch he choke. It doesn't work anyways and if you pull it you'll undo the jewjew rigging I did to keep it working," The farmer explained.

"Ah I see. Okay no problem," Max replied as he turned the key and tapped the gas. The truck started up with a rumble for a few seconds then started to idol a bit smoother. He wanted to know what was under the hood as it didn't sound normal. However it would have come off rude so he refrained from doing so.

"Thank you again Herald. I owe you one," he commented.

"No...this makes us even," the old man said as he tapped the door and smiled taking a step back. This was his queue as Max threw it in gear and let out the clutch slowly. He even forgot to apply gas, but it didn't seem to matter as the engine was so powerful, not to mention idling high, that it spun the tires. Probably because of the oil and dirt on the pavement, but that was still unclear. At the moment it was unimportant. What was, was the fact that he now had a means of getting to her and the dream had led the way. Zipping down the dirt road he made good time as he got onto the service road. It didn't take long to get on the highway and start heading towards the middle of nowhere. How he knew this nowhere could only be one thing. She told him, or more to the point he saw the paperwork all the people were walking around the room with in the dream. And in one such moment one of the assistants was ordering pizza and below the order form was the address of the place. Not to mention he had a built in compass pointing right at her in his head. He followed he compass for days without even stopping until the engine started to spit and sputter. Rolling to a stop he looked down to one of the few lights that was still working on the dash to see the gas gauge still said full.

"Great. I should have known that was wrong," Max said stepping out of the truck to look in the bed. In the bed was a tank with a pump arm on it and what sounded like sloshing fluids from the sudden stop. Opening the cap he took a whiff. It was an extra tank of gas. Pulling the nozzle from the bed he put it in the truck and then got up on the truck and started pumping the gas into the truck until it finally was full. Pulling the nozzle he let it drain until it was empty on the ground then threw it in the bed of the truck again and got back into the driver's seat. Turning the key over the truck struggled to start. It dragged over and over but didn't do more than a quick jerk then back to struggling again. Looking down he noticed he had accidentally hit the choke. Whatever the farmer had done was not not working. Perhaps he could figure it out, he thought. Stepping to the front of the truck he popped the hood and took a look. It was still early in the day so there was some light. Reaching down he saw what looked like a bottle cap that was melted to the engine block. That cap apparently was filling in the gap for something, but what? What could that farmer have possibly used that cap for to keep the engine running? It didn't make much sense. Stepping down from the trucks bumper he looked up to see flashing lights. Looking around the hood he saw a police officer walking up to him.

"Shit," he muttered to himself.

"What seems to be the problem?" the police officer asked. Max didn't want to draw attention to himself.

"Ah was just trying to get this truck home before the quick fix repair had worn out, but seems my luck didn't hold out," Max replied.

"Anything I can do to help?" the officer offered pointing his flashlight all around as he inspected the truck.

"Uhh, well do you happen to have a plastic bottle cap?" Max asked.

"A plastic bottle cap?" The skepticism was clear.

"Yeah I use it to hold the choke in place," Max was just making things up. He really didn't know if that was what the farmer had done, but since he was told about a quick fix for it he used that excuse to the officer as well. There was an awkward silence for a moment or two before the officer replied.

"Sure. Wait here," the officer added as he turned towards his car and headed back. After a brief wait he returned with a bottle cap just as max had asked. Max took a look at the choke assembly and the cap. Reaching out he tried to clip it to the choke but it popped off. He tried it several times before he finally pulled on the choke a bit then placed the cap on and it held. That was it. The cap kept the choke from pulling any further and was the reason why it idled so high. Satisfied that he had fixed it he stepped back and closed the hood brushing off his hands on one another. Looking back at the cop he saw he had his hand on his gun.

"You're not from around here are you?" asked the officer causing max to be nervous. Max's heart began to pump hard. He was going to be gunned down and never find his cat, he thought.

"No I'm not. I'm just passing through after I'm done here," Max answered. The tension built for a bit longer before the officer started to chuckle a bit.

"I knew it was you Isaac. Man I haven't seen you since you worked on my Ranch so many years ago. What brought you way out here? there isn't many ranches here or farms for that matter," The officer added as he hugged Max.

"Ah well like you said there aren't many, but I always find that one," Max chuckled back taking in a deep breath after the near scare.

"That is so true," The officer replied.

"Weren't you like a few states over? I remember you raising Longhorns or something like that," Max asked.

"Yeah I had a few. Didn't help my ranch much as they are the reason I lost my ranch in the first place,"

"Let me guess, they jumped your fences?" Max knew what the reason had to be considering how longhorns were.

"Yep! Damn things ran right out in the street and got hit by a car. I had to pay out so much when they sued me I don't even want to think about it. Anyways, I best get back to my job. Lots of serving and protecting to do. You have yourself a good day Isaac, don't work too hard," The officer said as he returned to the sound of his radio on his shoulder. The officer sat there talking to the radio for the moment while Max sat back down in the truck and started it up. That was the sound he expected. Idling high with no trouble of staying running. Max put it into gear and took off slowly as to not raise the officer's suspicions. Isaac. One of many names he was known for using. It was not his real name. In fact he hardly ever used his real name at all. It was easier to disappear from the grid if you made up a new name each time you stopped in a new town. It did get hard to figure out or remember what it was when you returned to that town. However it was the only way to keep from being tracked down. It wasn't that he was a criminal or any of the like, but it was his desire to stay hidden. Of course all of that would have to be addressed another time as he finally made it in front of an abandoned military base. All the signs and vehicles looked of a time long passed. The last time anything on the base had seen action Hitler was trying to take over the world. Pulling up to the hanger door of what looked like an airplane hanger, Max couldn't see anything that looked like there was any recent activity. Was his vision wrong? Maybe she was not in trouble after all. Turning off the truck he stepped out and walked up to the door on the side of the larger door. Reaching out to take hold of the knob he found it was locked, but not well. With a good shake he found it popped open easily. He began to walk in.

"I will take back my gift to you. You are not worthy," called out a voice. The voice was vaguely familiar. When he thought about it Max did indeed recognize it. It was the elf from when he was being held by the cats. Turn around quickly he saw the elf decked out in some crazy outfit he could only have gotten from his people.

"Uh, hey you, how's it going?" Max said stepping back from the door slowly almost tripping over several bars and other tools littered about on the ground.

"You will give me back the gift now," the elf demanded.

"Oh, sorry I don't have anything but Garliva's clothing and I just don't think it's yours style," Max kept his distance as the elf approached. Falling on his back Max grabbed a crowbar and swung at the elf as the elf caught it still reaching for his face. Before the elf could make contact Max kicked up as hard as he could making contact between the elf's legs. Then with his other leg while the elf was doubled over he pushed the elf away from his causing the elf to stumble a bit.

"You will regret that," the elf said reaching out his hands causing a glow to flow from his body into the air towards the elf. Before reaching the elf it darted off in another direction and around the buildings. "What?! NO!" The elf tried desperately to collect the energy but instead it went around him to where he could not touch it. After a short bit the energy flow just stopped and what was left went back into Max. The drain of energy had taken its toll on Max as he leaned up against the truck just trying not to collapse. Truly there was no way he was going to stop it from happening. Approaching with even more hatred than before the elf used his power to raise the metals around him in the air. Knowing the metal was likely to be used as a projectile he rolled to the side and struggled to his feet as he began to run. It was no use as each of the metal items struck him one at a time with great force.

"You dare to bond souls with a beast?! They are an abomination. And so is your bond. When I kill you there will be no bond and I will take it from her body with my bare hands," the elf threatened. Feeling a sudden need to act Max grabbed one of the flying metals in mid air and tossed it back with all his might. It flew straight at the elf stopping only inches from his face.

"Very well. This will be the instrument of your death," the elf explained as he shot the metal back faster then it was sent hitting Max in the leg with a loud crack. Max yelled out in agonizing pain.

******

Suddenly Garliva's eyes opened wide and her body was covered in the glowing light that had come from Max. The scientists all watched the glow shocked as they had no idea what it was or where it came from. Some ran in fear it was ghosts, while others argued there was a gas leak and they needed to clear the area. The head scientist stepped closer to her to get a closer look to be caught right in the path as she broke her bonds that held her. Jumping from the table through the scientist he found himself flat on his back as she ran over him. Watching her go he jumped up and tapped a few buttons on his tablet. The alarms rang out over the base alerting everyone to her escape. It seemed that since Max felt he was about to die he had released his energy to her. Garliva's awareness of him was heightened with this transfer of energy and as soon as his leg broke she could feel it. Running through the building she dodged back and forth through the people and soldiers before they could even react. When they doors were closing she would slide past them or toss nearby objects or people in order to stop them. Before anyone could do anything to recover her speed had led her to the final door were she slammed her shoulder into it and knocked it off its hinges. It only too moments for her to come upon the elf who was beating Max with bar over and over. Not thinking she snatched up a pipe off the ground and tossed it like a spear right through the elf's back as he was about to come down on Max again. Screaming the elf dropped his bar and gripped the pipe. Still striking the elf she knocked him off of Max and kneeled down over him. She was so focused on Max she never saw the pipe that struck her across the head. She rolled off of Max knocked out. The elf laughed as she kicked the cat while she was down on the ground. Then an evil smile covered his face as she kneeled down touching Garliva's head. Slowly she rose from the ground and stood before him.

"Good my slave. Kill that human," he ordered of her. Max struggled to get to his side as he looked at her.

"I said kill him," the elf said again pointing at Max. She turned very slowly. Her soul was being controlled by the elf.

"No," Max cried though busted lips. Fighting to get to his feet he took strike after strike she laid upon his flesh. Finally standing despite his broken leg he turned and dropped his body onto hers. The sound of his broken ribs creaking called out for all to hear. Garliva caught him as he held tight while she clawed his back. It only took moments before his body dropped into the celestial planes with her. In the pitch black starless back drop they met face to face with his head upon her chest. The stars in her body glowed faintly. His body had crimson growing over his back sides and face. His leg almost looked disconnected at how dark the red was in his leg that he broke. Max pulled away the best he could to look her in the eyes and stand up. He knew his body could feel the pain, but in this form any and all pain had to be caused on this plane before it was truly felt. All other pain from the real world was no more than the feeling of a limb that falls asleep. The purest white glow flowed from his eyes as he could feel the impact of a pipe outside the plane. He looked at her head as her head was started to change color from its normal to a purplish green that was spreading slowly. Taking his hand he pet the side of her face then drew his hand over her head as he focused on the infected area like he did when he removed the red stars before. On the side of his head it started to turn the same shade of purplish green just as her head was no longer growing in that color at the moment. Her eyes began to water in kind. His head now as much infected as hers, her head began to grow again. The purplish green color was about to consume their heads both. Closing her eyes in turn she reached up with both hands and started focusing on him. Feeling her energy as all the white stars began to glow even brighter he grunted from another impact out side their plane as he took his other hand and placed it on her as well. With both of them focusing so hard the glow grew so bright that they were completely non-visible.

Being blown back after striking Max one last time the Elf rolled several times upon the pavement.

"Tha hell!" He stated as he sat up. Before him the glow that was once only seen by Max and Garliva within their own planes flooded the real world causing the elf to cover his eyes. Removing his hand from his vision the elf was now before something unlike anything he had ever seen before. It was almost like a mixture of both Max and Garliva. A perfect blind that had both of their facial features and longer feet but not completely human and not completely a cat as she was. instead it had a smaller chest, less muscle mass than she had, and a shorter tail. Areas around their pelvis, chest and hands glowed so bright the details of the body in that area was not able to be seen. In all the whole body glowed brightly to where it was barely visible.

Lifting off the ground new being formed of the two floated over to the elf who was now trying to scramble for his dear life only to be caught by the neck. Lifted up off the ground the new being spoke without moving its lips.

"You have given a gift that has brought together two worlds that could never see eye to eye in any amount of time. For that we are grateful. But now you strike us in an attempt to kill us both to take that gift back. We cannot allow that. But we will not kill you for these actions. No. Instead we shall give you a gift in return. We will give back to you the pain and suffering you have given us," with that the new being's arm glowed brighter and brighter with sparks coming off of it like that of an electric welder. The sparks seared the ground with each touch. The being's arm had colors of red to purplish green that flowed through their arm into the elf who screamed as if being tortured. The screams were blood curdling. Then in one final act the glow of the new being and the elf got so bright neither form could be seen.

Just as quick as it had begun the light disappeared and the three forms were themselves again. Max and Garliva were panting heavily, while the elf's eyes were rolled back in his head and his body quiver. Arching his feet the elf bent back his head falling to the ground writhing. Both Max and Garliva stood with not a stitch of clothing upon their body. At Max's feet lay the clothing he had been wearing. Of course Garliva was not clothed before hand anyways. Looking at each other neither one was truly sure what had happened. Never had either one of them felt that close to another being as they had just then. Upon the ground the elf had other problems to worry about as he was being crushed mentally by his own mind control and every brake, bruise and injury that Max and Garliva was dealt had been transferred onto the elf's body. The physical and psychological damage was so great that his body finally just gave up and he exhaled his last breath while Max and Garliva watched. What had they done? Or was it really them who did it? All questions they were asking themselves. Looking over his shoulder Max saw the man in the business suit walking their way with soldiers pointing their guns at them. Taking hold of the cat he pulled her out of the way as bullets began to fly. Tripping Garliva caught Max's clothing with her foot. Picking it up with her hand as they hid behind the truck she passed them to him.

"Thanks, but I think we are going to have to make a break for it," he explained to her as the sirens of a police car met their ears.

"What's going on?" Called out the police.

"Wait! that's the officer I just talked to not long ago," Max said trying to peak around the corner of the truck to see who it was.

"This is a military affair. Get back in your car and leave filth," said the man in the suit. That was enough to set the officer off. See this as his opportunity Max made his way back to the passenger door of the truck opening it slowly and as quiet as possible directing Garliva to get in.

"My cloths," she said keeping low.

"Yeah you left them with the farmer apparently," Max said as he crowd into the truck over and around her body getting to behind the wheel of the truck. Knowing he had only one chance to get the truck started and take off he took a deep breath making sure not to bump the choke like last time. Turning so he could easily sit up once the truck was started he pressed the breaks and pushed in the clutch. Taking one last breath he turned the key to have the truck start quickly. The sound of bullet hail rang out as it first hit the truck then started heading another direction. They were apparently being fired upon by the officer and they were firing back. Throwing it in gear he popped the clutch and sat up pulling the steering wheel towards the group of soldiers causing them to have to stop shooting at the officer and run for cover. Doing half a donut Max whiped the truck around and headed towards the officer to watch him make it back to his car injured.

Both the truck and police car took off as fast as possible back down the road that had led them there. Looking in the rear view mirror on his door he could see his friend swerving back and forth. What was strange was there were no cars following them. This was bad.

"That is strange," Max said out loud.

"Agre'. Ef nou fall'o," Garliva said as she looked out the small back window of the cab. Vibration in the truck started to seem familiar. Before they could brace for impact the truck was thrusted into the range of a rocky side as Max turned as best as possible glancing off the rocks. Stopping as soon as he hit he watched the squad car plow head on to the rock disabling the car. In a rush Max threw on his clothing as fast as possible save for the boots. Jumping out of the car he ran over to the officer that had been hit in the face with the airbag. Max was worried that he had been knocked out only to find a gun pointed at him when he opened the door.

"It's me!" Max called out raising his hands out of a quick reaction.

"Isaac. I can't move," the officer said lowering his gun while holding his side.

"Let me get you out of there," Max told his friend as he reached in pulling the best he could. Suddenly extra hands grabbed the officer helping him pull the officer free. Looking up Max met eye to eye with Garliva. Nodding both smiled as they laid the officer on the ground. Garliva went to work looking at the blood that was coming from the officer's right side.

"He urt, but nou bad," She explained as she started digging in the hole to pull out the bullet.

"Not bad my a...," The officer started when he noticed what Garliva was, "Do I even want to know what she is?" The officer looked her up and down. Clothed again in her original attire she was not like anything he had seen before.

"This is Garliva...she has saved my life many times," Max said smiling at her with her smile coming back at him. The officer patted Max on the arm.

"Thank you, and your friend."

"Wilcom," Garliva answered as she reached out her hand and took the officers in her own. Both Max and her lifted the officer to his feet. Looking his shirt over he pulled it open to find his body armor had taken too many bullets to be used much more. He was lucky. With all the training the fact was the officer should have been dead.

"I think I saw my life flash before my eyes," the officer said.

"I was wondering why you fired upon them," Max asked.

"I could see you two were unarmed. That is not legal, military or not," the officer replied.

"True. We are grateful for your assistance," Max answered as he looked around. This was not like the world Garliva came from. No. This was something far worse. The calls and cries of vicious animals and monsters echoed around them. Their voices had a strange resonance like the sound of tapped crystal glasses. Now they would have to fight for survival together.

Chrysalis

Max and Garliva were greatly interested in this new world. At first glance it was thought to be just normal dirt, rock, various vegetation and more, but it was more, like glass. Looking at the rock Max bounced off of with the truck they noticed it was like a dark brown glass. When Max touched where he hit it cut his fingers causing them to bleed from the razor sharp edges. Looking down Max looked at his feet to see shards of the glass type rock all over, and a pool of blood that was gathering there. The bottom of his feet had been cut by the glass and he had not even noticed.

"You nid sit truck," Garliva stated as she took his arm and walked him back to the tail gate. Pulling the leaver she patted it to indicate for him to get up on it.

"Where did you find her?" the officer asked still holding his side.

"She found me," Max said giving a smile.

"Found you huh?" The officer scoffed.

"Fond tu kill you. Thaut you ef. Fond you betta'. You mor," she explained. Max snickered a bit at how she would piece the words together with what sounded like cat noises to speak. Drawing the attention away from the conversation the officer went to the truck of his car. Inside he pulled a red bag with a white cross.

"Hey cat...thing...person you. Use this,"

"I Garliva," she replied.

"Garliva...Use this," the officer offered holding it out to her before continuing, "You will find the wraps and bandages you will need to take care of both of your feet." Both Max and Garliva looked down to see there was a small pool of blood coming from her feet too. Looking at each other with Max's turn to be stern he used his finger to motion for her to sit on the tailgate too. Sighing she placed the bag down between them and sat. Opening the bag the two started pulling out what they would need and doctoring their own feet than each other. Almost as if they had a well orchestrated plan that they were using to bandage each other up. The officer found this to be very odd, but said no words. Knowing that Max had boots or at least some sort of footwear, he went to the driver side of the truck and pulled his boots from the seat. Garliva however must not have brought anything footwear wise as he way nothing. With both their feet wrapped they smiled at each other when Max's boots hung between the two.

"I'm guessing these are max's," The offer stated. Max took them from him and started putting them on over his bandages.

"There doesn't seem to be anything that she can wear and she can't just walk around without something to protect her from the glass," The officer pointed out. Max placed his finger to his chin in deep thought when the sight of tire tread that had come off a blown tire gave him an idea. The tire tread looked new but somehow got hit causing it to blow. Glancing around the back of the truck as he stood in the bed Max grabbed a broke saw. It wouldn't be perfect but it would protect her feet. With determination driving him, Max took hold of the tire tread and started sawing at it wildly.

"What are you doing Isaac," The officer asked confused completely.

"Leona'd...Leo...na..rd," She corrected while she watched. Max paused for a moment in his actions. So she learned his real name. Must have been from when they were connected. Taking up his task again he cut a piece from the tread then turned to line it up to the bottom of Garliva's foot. The tread was perfect for protecting the bottom of her toes and foot pad she had but also went up the back of her foot towards the haunches as well.

"Your real name is Leonard? I thought you said Isaac?" The officer was visibly upset. Going back to cut another piece Max sawed wildly again.

"My real name is Leonard. I have been wondering about helping farmers and ranchers for the better part of twenty five years. I did not want to be found so each time I worked for someone new I gave a different name. Never the same name twice," Max explained as he pulled a new piece from the tread and turned to find it was not a perfect match to the first tread but both would protect her foot bottoms well. Taking out the medical tape he started to tape on the treads to the bottom of her foot. He made sure it was tight enough it wouldn't slide but loose enough that it wouldn't cut off her circulations.

"I can't believe it. I guess it makes sense but what are you running from?" the officer asked while Garliva tested out her mobility with her new footwear.

"A horror I can never undo," Was all max said as he stood up in the bed of the truck and assisted Garliva to her feet. She moved her legs and pressed her feet to the tread testing how they bent and moved getting a feel for how they would work when she walked.

"Well you be sure and tell me when finally feel up to it. You owe me at least that much," the officer informed.

"Sure thing Roger," Max said as she jumped off the truck and helped Garliva down.

"Good," was all the officer could say as he walked around to take a look at the front of the truck. Max walked around Garliva as she collected the rest of the medical supplies into the red bag, then grabbing it and following.

"Looks like all you did was bust out a light. We should be able to still run," the officer reported as he opened the hood looking down to find the bottle cat had popped up but was still pretty close to being in place. Reaching over the officer set it back the way Max had it before then closed the hood. Motioning Garliva into the truck cab he followed after and closed the door.

"Lets go. We need to get moving before we find out what those screams were earlier," Max stated.

"Sure but let me grab my stuff first," Walking back to his car, the officer grabbed a bag from the back of his trunk along with an assault rife. Then as he walked passed the driver door he reached in pulling out the laptop, a flat folded panel of sorts and his shotgun. Tossing the duffle bag in the back of the truck he lifted the gate and walked around to the passenger side. Shutting the door he placed the computer next to him and the shotgun between his legs propped up against the dash.

"Okay lets go," the officer ordered reaching for a seat belt only to find the truck was too old to have one. "I guess it's safe to say there are no airbags."

"Ai' bug..s..." Garliva uttered a bit confused because Max's memories did not show her such things.

"Airbags. Bags. They will pop out when you hit things to keep you from getting hurt," Max explained only to have the officer cut him off.

"No they don't keep you from getting hurt, the keep you from getting severely hurt."

"Oh, yeah that," Max dismissed as he turned the key starting the engine. Reaching for the shifter right in front of Garliva he made his best effort to shift without hitting her with it too much. It brought back memories of when his grandfather and grandmother were alive. They would sit next to each other in the truck and were so close to each other his parents would tease them by calling them 'the two-headed monster'. Of course it was only because it bothered his grandmother. Reaching up with her arm nearest Max she gently took hold of his arm to comfort him.

"It's okay. Just remembering my grand parents having a truck like this. They use to sit close to each other when going down the road," Max's words trailed off as he started to drive. He could feel the warmth that came from her body due to their close proximity. Probably not unusual, he thought, as she is covered in fur.

Not wanting to risk wrecking again Max kept his speed low as he followed the weaving glass structures around them. The sun started to go beyond the horizon only to have the glass around them begin to glow from the light passing through them. It was light day again even though it was night. It was the most bizarre thing they had ever seen. What made it worse was they noticed some of the glass structures were moving. Almost like a glass dog, or lizard or something. It was unclear exactly what it was that darted off between the rock like glass and the glass like green tree shaped objects that came into view. Slowing moving his hand to his shotgun the officer prepared for an ambush while Max tried to roll up his window that was clearly off its track.

"That's not good," Max muttered in response to his window not completely going up.

"Don't worry about that just keep driving," the officer demanded as he positioned the shotgun to fire out the window. Across their path all sorts of wolf like glass creatures dashed back and forth. Unable to miss them all Max plowed right through one as the sound of glass flying everywhere could be heard. The impact caused the truck to swerve a bit, but didn't seem to do much damage otherwise.

"I hit one!" Max said as he tried to avoid the others a bit better. Soon there were too many to count more or less avoid hitting. Skidding to a stop he held the breaks. Not a word was uttered between them as the sight of so many glass wolves were around them that you could not see the ground anymore nor a pathway out. All of them snarling and growling as they got closer. The sound as if the growl was coming from the inside of a glass bottle made the three want to cover their ears. Garliva looked for something to use as a weapon only to find a screwdriver that she passed to Max. She went for the claw weapon she had used before but found it missing. She must have dropped it in the barn when she was protecting Max. Reaching around under the seat she found a small hatchet. The three readied their weapons only to watch all the glass wolves turn sharply with their pointy ears perked over to the right somewhere. Something had spooked them, Max thought as the entire pack of glass wolves started running off. A few in the end not making it away as they were hit by dark purple almost black glass humanoids were attacking them causing the wolves to shatter into pieces. What remained would continue to struggle until all of the shiny fluids finished spilling from the broken parts. Opening his door Max turned off the truck and killed the lights as the sun was in the sky. No sooner did Max step on the ground that one of the glass people turned on him. Before Max could do anything the officer Blew it away with the shotgun. This seemed to have shocked them as they all paused. They looked back to what seemed like a much larger one of them. He had his hand raised.

"Leave and you won't loose anymore," the officer ordered. Max looked down at the body that had just broken from the shot. All the internal organs were some kind of glass. The food that was in it's stomach was more like sand or something of the like. His blood pooled around him and as soon as it was out started to harden. As it hardened it changed colors to something near the color of it's outer glass. Crawling out the same side as Max she stood beside him in as much awe as he was at the creatures before them. Neither of them had seen anything like it in their life.

"Forgive us," the glass people's leader called back with the same eary echo as the wolves. Opening his door the officer jumped out of the truck still holding the shotgun at the ready.

"What did you say?" The officer asked.

"Forgive us I say. We have been fighting the Shard Straves for so long we do not know what to do when a new comes about. And as you saw one of our own will attack to protect us," the glass people's leader understood their words from what little he heard or they used the same language for some odd reason.

"Why did you attack those glass wolves?" Max asked motioning in the direction the glass wolves had gone.

"Glass wolves? Yes wolves does sound appropriate for them," Their leader answered in thought before continuing. "I shall explain, but first let us show you our hospitality with an invite to feast with us. Come we have much to discuss," The leader hardly taking his eyes off the shotgun the whole time. Looking at each other the three could not think of a reason not to accept their offer.

"Okay we will follow you in our tr..." Max started to explain only to be cut off.

"No need for your contraption. Our village is not accessible to such beasts," The leader said as they walked back into the trees and one by one disappeared.

"Uh yeah sure why not," Max said as the three huddled around each other.

"Max what are you doing?"

"Excellent. To the feast," the leader said as he started walking in the same direction. Three started to follow while still having their conversation.

"What are you doing? We don't know if they are hostile," the officer interjected.

"Yess, we nou 'ave chance the' attack us," Garliva had been studying the new people and how dangerous they would be in a fight.

"I know but we can't survive an attack of that many wolves either," Max said as he paused to look over his shoulders to find a single glass wolf was watching them, weaving and bobbing about with it's glowing eyes. The officer and Garliva looked back only to have the wolf get out of sight before either could glimpse a look at it as well. Letting go for the moment they followed the glass people through the trees made of glass.

Each blade of grass and tree leaf was razor sharp cutting them if they got too close. By time the small group had made it to where they were being led Max's pant legs were nearly in shreds up to the calves. Garliva had blood that was coming from the cuts causing her fur to mat. The officer too barely had pant legs below the knees. Clearing the glass trees there was a glass bowl like opening in the middle almost like the glass had flowed like a wave of ocean at one time then dried. The forms below their feet made amazing designs only glass could do. Light hit anywhere on the surface and it shimmered like a disco ball. Stepping on it, the three could feel their feet threatening to slip upon the smooth glass surface. Only the shapes made in the wave like pattern kept them from falling. In the middle of the impact crater was all the evidence one needed to understand why there was a wave of glass in the first place. A large hunk of rock sunk into the glass nearly the whole way. The people of glass had built their structures around the meteor and into it. Within their walls were pools of liquid that they had never seen before. Around it the glass people cut the meteor in order to make a large bowl like shape to contain the liquid. Max watched as he saw glass shards were help together and dunk into the liquid then came out crying as if it was just born. This was how they created their new generation. Mean while Garliva saw the injured dip their injury into the liquid and it would seal leaving an almost transparent sealing of glass. Those that had drained out all their fluids from the inside were chipped away with fashioned stones that were pieces of the meteor to create new glass shards which they would dip and create new people. The officer on the other hand was more nervous about the fact the glass people were weapons without even having to try or use any objects at all.

"Please join us. We feast on the other side," announced the larger glass being as the others cheered. Getting into a sort of queue they pilled out on the opposite side that they had come in to table like sand boxes that they all walked up to. Each spacing out far enough to give room for all of them to fit. Max, Garliva and the officer stood there looking down at the sand like the others. The leader made a point to stand on the opposite side of the table.

"Please," motioned the leader to the three.

"What? You expect us to eat sand?" the officer commented.

"This is probably what they eat. We mustn't be rude," Max whispered to the officer. Garliva leaned towards the other two.

"A'k tu eat," she suggested, not that the officer understood her even though Max did.

"Fine, whatever," the officer took a hand off the gun and reached down into the sand taking in a palm full and bringing it to his lips. Max and Garliva did the same. Almost choking on the sand the officer almost spit it out but remembered what Max and Garliva said. Muscling through the grit he swallowed his bite. Max and Garliva both could not believe he actually at some as they merely faked it just as Garliva had said. Not able to address it as they would offend their host Max turned his attentions to the leader.

"So how did this large meteor get here?" he asked.

"It is glass womb. It brings life to us all. Except the beasts of the Shard Fields. They are born of darkness and death. We seek to rid our world of their foul fangs," the leader said only to have the officer pipe in.

"here here," the officer was now stuffing his mouth with handfuls of the sand as if it was an all you could eat buffet.

Garliva looked at Max. Max hardly shared a glance at her as he knew there was nothing he could do at that point in time.

"Where I come from creatures like that exist as well. Over generations we tamed them and they became excellent companions and help. Have you considered domesticating a few of them?" Max asked as all the eating including the officer stopped and they all looked at the leader.

"Hmm, I had not thought of that. Yes that is what we will do. Max how would you like to be my second in command. All take orders from you, and you will have her as your shimmer," the leader asked pointing to Garliva as her opposite.

"Uhh, what?"

"He's saying you would be his second in command and that cat thing would be yours to command," the officer picked up eating again.

"Okay, how do you know that is what he's saying, and more importantly how did he know my name. I never said," Max started only to be interrupted.

"Just eat your food. We all need to be of one mind," the officer said as in mid bite he looked over at Max and Garliva positioning his shotgun to the ready.

"Food giv mind tu cente'r," Garliva stepped back pulling Max with her.

"This isn't a village it's a cult. The Meteor gives you control over anyone who eats the sands that is contaminated by the radiation from the meteor," Max gasped. A smile came over the leader's face as he crossed his arms. The officer turned from looking at the leader as he pointed the shotgun at Max and

Garliva. Silvery glass like lines line veins crossed his face and hands. The glass people started climbing over and under the tables heading for Max and Garliva. Knowing that the meteor was very important Max pushed Garliva into the door as she almost fell. Behind the wall they kept in sight of the pool of water in the middle as well as positioning to escape out the other door. Each time the officer tried to aim they would duck, but they couldn't escape the glass people easy. Seeing their end in site they held each other only to hear the shattering of glass. Looking up they found one of the glass wolves looking at them only inches from their face.

"You need to follow me if you want to live," the glass wolf instructed as waves of his fellow wolves flooded into the meteor biting and scratching all the glass people they could giving Max and Garliva the ability to run. Following the wolf they had just talked to they chased the waving tail behind the glass canine. Once out of site of the meteor deep within the trees of glass they looked back to find nothing was following them. Or was it. The rumble like a herd came up behind them as the fight had followed the glass beings into the field of glass trees as well.

"Move!" the glass wolf cried tugging on Max's pant legs. The wolf ran in front of them shattering all the glass grass and leaves in their way. The running kept on for what seemed like hours until the wolf finally stopped and turned to sit down. Panting the two braced themselves on their knees as they tried to catch their breath.

"Why...are you....helping us?" Max asked of the wolf.

"Because you are not of the cult," The wolf replied.

"You watch?" Galiva asked as both of them stood up.

"Yes I..." the wolf doubled over as if in pain before continuing. "My brothers are being hurt."

"How do you know that?" Max asked.

"Because they are my brothers. Do you not see and feel what your brothers feel?" the wolf asked.

"No that is not something we can do," Max explained.

"We...du," Garliva said looking Max in the eyes.

"That's true, but it's...not something we normally do," Max added.

"I see. Well my brothers and I..." the wolf stood and went silent as glass wolves returned bleeding the fluids of glass they had seen before and others completely another color then they were before they left. Max and Garliva watched as they were surrounded by all the wolves. Most of the wolves still their original color were bleeding out and just laid down to die. The new wolves were as if they had not fought at all or had white marks like scars like that the glass people had when they were healed. Their color of a purple color showing they had been dipped in the meteor waters. The three knew they were surrounded by the dead and dying.

"I think it's time I no longer have brothers. We must leave. NOW!" the wolf cried turning as he bounced off the trees to keep out of reach of the other wolves. Garliva and Max had to do hurdles around and over the snapping wolves to get free. Making a mad dash the three ran towards the sound of a water fall. It had an odd crystal type ring to it.

"What ever you do don't drink the water, and jump!" the wolf said as it jumped from the cliff. Without pausing the two jumped after the wolf holding their breath. The other wolves that gave chase turned back and walked away.

As Max and Garliva hit the water it wasn't normal. Their feet buckled as if they had hit something almost solid as concrete but yet flowed like jell-o. Max did as he was told and held his breath as best he could but he was unable to fight the sinking in the thickened waters. Falling deeper and deeper he found his leg being pulled hard off into the far direction from the surface, and the falls. releasing bubbles little at a time he finally was running out of air and needed to come up soon or he would not be able to survive. Still fighting the urge he was about to gasp for air when he broke the surface to find him and Garliva were being dragged by their clothing. Garliva by the strap of her top and him bit his pant leg. The pair wiped themselves off of the heavy water looking at the wolf then at the cliff they had just leapt from.

"Here we shall be safe," the glass wolf looked at the other side almost morning his loss. Reaching out to pat the wolf's side only to find he cut himself upon the hide of the wolf.

"Seems your flesh is quite fragile. Where are you from?" The wolf asked turning his gaze to Max.

"I frowm Rradirma vill'ge," Garliva said. The wolf turned to her.

"Ah I see. Seems your village is very diverse in appearance," the wolf said.

"Kinda...I'm actually from United States," Max interjected.

"I see. So this is not your mate?" the wolf asked of Max causing him and Garliva to look at each other.

"Uhh, no we are not," Max replied. Looking between them the wolf squinted his red eyes carefully.

"I see. Then this bond of energy...Is that something that is normal between you to?" the wolf's words stumped them both as Max blushed and Garliva's eyes grew. Seemed neither of them even knew of the energy. "I suppose not. Well we can't stay here. My brothers will be back and considering they are under the control of our enemy I'm sure we will be easy pickings if we don't move."

Standing up Max helped Garliva to her feet. The ground was not like above as the cliff was covered in glass everything. While down at the bottom there were some glass things but it was all solid rock like you would find near a volcano. But that wasn't their focus as Max and Garliva both pondered on their connection. It was clear it all started as of the green mist that affected Max. The question was how far did the mist affect them and what else did it have in store.

"What happened to the other glass wolves like you?" Max asked trying to turn his thoughts away from his current concern.

"Glass wolves? Hmm, that...I like that yes I am a Glass Wolves,"

"Wolf. One is wolf. Many is Wolves," Max corrected.

"Wolf. Even better. To answer your question they were corrupted by the Water of Possession. They are no longer my brothers," The wolf explained.

"Which would have happened to us if we had drank that pool we were just in right?" Max asked further. Garliva just as intently paying attention to each and every word spoken by the wolf.

"No," He replied without pausing in his stride.

"Den Why you till us hol' breath?" Garliva pipped in.

"Because it would have changed your body into a glass wolves,"

"You min wolf?" Garliva added.

"Yes wolf. See a simple stone tossed in becomes the mind of my wolves. Their body forms from the Waters of Awakening. When any thing that is living falls in it will do nothing as long as they don't breathe it in. Even I would be reborn again if I was to swallow enough and loose who I am and know to the new that I would be come.

"Huh that's..." Max started only to hear yelling in the distance. It was directed at them.

"You can't hide Max! I am of the Glass People and you will join us or die!" the voice called out. It was familiar but with the sound that the glass creatures had when they talked. It was the officer.

"Nou!" Garliva said as she and Max looked up to see the officer jump from the cliff into the water with several of the wolves.

"They turned him into glass," Max commented as they were stuck staring at the new officer.

"Watching them come will not prevent what they are planning to do to us once they get here," The wolf said trying to get their attention. Emerging from the waters Green and Purple wolves shook off the waters and looked at each other.

"Wait!" the wolf said stepping before Max and Garliva. "My brothers are returning. We must get them all back into the water!" Said the wolf as he took off at a full on dash at the purple glass wolves.

"My brothers push them into the waters until they drink of it," He said flailing his body towards a purple wolf pushing him back into the waters. Max and Garliva took off at a run at a few wolves but got blocked by the officer. All skin on his body was made of glass of a rose with a hint of gray in color. Both Max and Garliva could see the shotgun and knew he would use it. A wicked smile crossed his face as he started to lift the gun. Before he could shoot the gun several green wolves jumped up biting down on the arms of his clothing which echoed with the sound of cracking glass as it fell away from his body.

Backing into the fray Garliva and Max were fighting to keep from being attacked by the purple wolves. Each time they pushed the wolves towards the water they turned to fight back keeping Max and Garliva at bay. Green wolves jumped in each time it seemed like they were about to be bitten. Jumping free of the action Garliva Turned back to watch the fight as it spread all over the shores of the waters. Max Saw Garliva had gotten free of the fight and decided to do the same only to be grabbed by the collar and tossed into the water. Holding his breath just in time he found his body went straight to the bottom. Standing up he was up to the waters to his waist. He was about to head back to shore when he remembered that the waters turned the purple wolves green when they drank the waters. Which had showed great results as Max watched the last few purple wolves being tossed in the waters. Give a smirk to his idea max would wait for the officer to closer. Slowly the officer sunk in the water to his ankle, then his knee and further and further while Max stayed just out of reach. Once it got to his waist Max turned to the glass wolves who were creeping in slowly.

"NOW GLASS WOLVES!" Max yelled as all the glass wolves jumped on the officer causing him to stumble. Max tried his best to move as fast as possible out of the way and around the flurry of glass creatures. Finally making it free he stood beside Garliva and looked back to watch the officer thrash about in the waters like something he had seen in a movie as a kid. After a bit all but one wolf had disappeared below the waters with the officer. Turning back to him the glass wolf spoke.

"Thank you. We may not have saved your friend but at least I have my brothers. Thank you," The wolf informed with the utmost sincerity. One by one the glass wolves broke the surface of the waters walking out as if they had never been in a fight only to sit next to the green wolf that stood behind. Once every last wolf was out of the water the officer emerged from the surface with a bright rosy color all in glass. All of his uniform held a brilliant blueish glow as well. The green wolf that stayed on sure walked over to the officer that looked down at it while it stared back. Sitting down the wolf bowed its head. The officer reached over to pet the wolf who's head cam up to this waist.

"Thank you for releasing me from that nightmare my new friend," the officer said as he looked back at Max. Max did not know if he should run or stay when the officer approached him.

"Seems that I can no longer go home. These wolves have been fighting the goblins monsters for years possibly centuries. They need my help to survive," the officer's words echoed like the wolves.

"I don't understand," Max said confused of it it. Turning back the officer began to explain.

"Over a million years ago the planet was as it is at your feet. Dead no life and never would. That meteor you saw caused everything to glass. When it leaked the liquids within it gave life to the glass. Those that were born here became free spirit glass creatures. Wolves. Those that were of the radiated sands..." The officer turned back to Max before continuing, "Became glass goblins." Max and Garliva's jaws dropped. Such a thing was impossible in any world due to physics and the rules of science. But here they were. Some even nudged upon Garliva and Max in respect for help. A proof of their existence and possibilities that could not be denied.

"Though I was unable to see it before I see it now. You both are bound to the same fate," The officer now of glass started only to have the ground rumble near them were there was no glass at all.

"We to leev we go now!" Garliva yelled at Max.

"Sorry have to go," Max called back to the officer before taking off in a full sprint behind the cat. It was only a matter of seconds before Garliva was within the circle in a complete stop reaching back for Max. Just barely touching tips Garliva gripped onto his hand and jerked him into the circle with her causing him to land on her. The sudden drop left them covered in small rocks and dirt. Opening their eyes it was clear they were no longer in the land of glass beings.

Chapter 10

Scales

Coughing both Garliva and Max said nothing at first. Too worried they would have dropped in another dark situation. This time it seemed more literal as all they could see was a single source of light that shined down upon them in a dark area. The ground seemed flat below them and covered in dust. Rolling onto his side Max sat up to look upon the light. Garliva sat up to do the same. Was there anything living in there with them? He couldn't see them. The cat next to him sniffed the air. Grimacing she covered her nose with her hand.

"Uh, that gross," she said as Max tried to stand only to find there was a low ceiling above them.

"Ouch!" he cried out.

"Wha't?!" Afraid of what might have hurt Max.

"Nothing, just...we don't have a lot of room to move it seems. Feeling with his hands he crawled a small circle around them to find the space for them to move around was only three body lengths long. The ceiling was a bit higher and more jagged where the light was coming through but all else smooth. As he crawled he could feel rocks as if they were chipped off of something larger scattered all about.

"Well, we seem to have gotten away from the world of glass but we are deeper into trouble than before," he explained to her as he looked around. She on the other hand drew her knees to her chest wrapping her arms around them.

"Tha'...volf say we...mmm, I do nou word for it," Garliva tried to ask only to find as far as her english had progressed she was still struggling.

"I'm sorry I'm not sure what you are asking," Max wrinkled his brow in confusion. Scooting her bottom closer she dropped her legs to sit with them crossed below her. Reaching out she grabbed both his hands and lifted them in her own. At that moment it became clear what she meant.

"Ah, you mean together as in, serious relationship," he said looking for clarification.

"Yes, and nou. What volf say mean more," She explained though it really did mean the same thing. What she was really trying to say was something a kin to marriage, and Max knew it.

"Probably because we don't seem to go far from each other. When you are in trouble I...I feel....it," Max stumbled upon his words. They were true. Hard for him to admit but all the same something he had not really thought about until that very moment.

"Dis relationship can nou make famly. Nou to say my people can nou have you...," Nodding her head touching his chest in the center then her own. "I one. Nou," she explained. It was something he was aware of as well. Such a match could not happen.

"That may be true but does that apply to us as we can be one?" catching himself trying to fight for something he felt was wrong he could not explain why the thought even crossed his mind in the first place. The though alone made him blush. Thinking it was best not to think of it he turn his side to her drawing away his hands. Garliva started to reach for him only to have him raise his hand.

"No. That is not necessary," he told her as now it was his turn to sit up with his knees to his chest. In his mind it was clear, having her around was warping his mind and soon he would be like those furries that he saw on TV. Vile degenerates that think of animals as life partners. It was clear he had to separate from her quickly before he was lost within the folds of the weird.

For hours they sat there saying and doing nothing. Not for reasons of her own choice where Garliva was concerned but each time she even thought about Max it was like he could sense it. She in turn could sense his desire to stay from her. They went on this way until finally they laid to rest. Max being the first one to fall completely asleep. Leaning up she looked over at him. Knowing he was asleep she crept over to him slowly making as little noise as possible. Poised over his body she looked down upon him when she noticed her strap was still not holding. The fact that part of her chest was not supported caused her to blush. But why? This was not something her people worried about. It was only to protect sensitive areas on their bodies from being scratched by plants and such was the only reason they wore anything in the first place. If it wasn't for that they would go without them all together. Surely it was because of Max. His mind connecting with hers has made her aware of these things, and by god she would have more. Touching his shoulder to turn him towards her, she closed her eyes as he opened his. Her mouth opened before his so quickly that he could not stop the merge of them both.

This time when he looked down to his hands he found his hands glowed more than they had previously. Looking up to her he saw her in the same pose she was in as he opened his eyes from being woken. Her stars were even brighter than before. Wrapping her arms around him he felt the warmth surround him only the edges of his feet and ears could feel the touch of cold. Where their bodies met being warmer than others. The feeling was far more intense than he had ever experienced before. His heart beat started to quicken as panic came over him. The both of them felt a tremor over and over growing in power as it hit them. Abruptly they were knocked out of their connection as they both ducked to prevent the small rocks and dust from injuring them. Looking up he watched as Garliva was pulled off of him and dragged out of the hole where the light came from only to have it darken in the room again as he was pulled out with her to a world lush and green with large rocks sticking up in the trees at what seemed random.

"Don't worry. We can survive this," a voice said in his head.

"Survive this? survive what? we are out numbered," Shaking his head he thought to himself. He must be crazy "I'm loosing my mind, there is no way that Garliva could be in my head. Get a grip I have to stay focus."

"What are you talking about? I am talking to you. I'm not sure how but I am," Garliva had indeed linked directly into his head.

"What? Why did you do this? My thoughts are my own?" He called out in front of all.

"Nou ask this. Jus' happen," She replied. The large lizard type creatures looked back and forth from each other puzzled at their arguing.

"Why do you have an accent when I hear you with my ears but none when I hear you in my head?" Max's words caused her to notice as well.

"Nou't Nou. I say right in min' hard say...mmm," She motioned as if it was coming from her mouth.

"It's harder to say from my mouth than it is to say directly to your heart," She told him in his head.

"This is going to be annoying," he muttered aloud. Not saying another word Max focused on not thinking anything as well. But he didn't need to as feelings flowed from him to her. Feelings that caused her face to stay in an almost perma-shock.

The feelings he was feeling were almost hateful towards her, a desire to get as far from her as possible as if she was the cause of all his blight. Despite herself her eyes began to water until she thought more about it. It must be a sign of strength and he was trying to keep up an image in front of the lizards.

Max and Garliva were dragged all the way in front of an aztec type stone chair with various primitive carvings along its surface. In the seat sat a large lizard with wings adorn with tons of precious metals and jewels. Tentacle like hair wiggled around his head and down his back a bit braided and held with gold rings.

Being tossed down before the dragon Max and Garliva were barely able to sit on their knees before them. Garliva though had their attention as most women of their village could only be noticed as female by a narrower snout. One of the dragon females kneeled down before her and examen the feminine appendages upon her chest. Starting to reach for them the dragon's hand was slapped away as Garliva did not feel it was their right to just touch. The dragon leader stood up pointing at Garliva.

"Take that thing out of my sight," he spouted in a booming voice. Looking down to Max the dragon looked between the two for a moment. It was the same look the glass goblin had at the site of Max and Garliva. This meant only one thing, the dragon too thought they were of the same species and how odd it was they were so much different from each other.

"You will fight our honor guard for the honor of your mate. If you loose you both die," Said the dragon as he stepped down from the throne and walked to a clearing in the village. There max was tossed in the middle and another dragon came in stabbing a staff in the ground. All the others did the same in a circle around them. Seemed regardless if he wanted too or not it was now time to fight.

Looking over his shoulder at the dragon leader Max only stood as tall as his calf of his leg. This guy was huge by any description. Though the larger dragon wasn't the threat as Max barely avoided the attack from the smaller dragon. The claws breezed by as Max fell backwards. Scrambling to his feet he squared off with the dragon. Which was far taller than he was. Had to be a good foot or two taller. Covered from top to bottom with polished scales and armor. Most of the other dragons wore nothing except for a the few that had bags or scraps of leather skins that covered their shoulders and heads. Likely to keep them from sunburning as the covered lizards were pale in color.

Moving to the side Max narrowly missing another lunge. From within the crowd Garliva made her way to the edge but as soon as she was to try and get in the ring too she was pulled back and down by the horde around her. She would not be assisting Max this time. He would have to survive on his own.

The fight carried on with Max getting sliced from time to time as he was not fast enough to avoid all the attacks. Each cut burned a new as it was certain there was some added effect he was unaware of. Fighting was starting to wear Max out he could hear a small nagging in the back of his mind.

"Dodge," it called to him. Looking up he noticed the lizard attacking almost as if he was in slow motion. Max turned to the side as the voice in his head called again, "Grab his wrist and strike his elbow." Max did as it said. A loud pop echoed around the group as they all gasped. The lizard's arm went limp to his side. Reaching over with his other arm he twisted it and pulled then an even louder snap followed. Flexing his hand on that arm it was clear he had relocated it back in its socket. Apparently tired of dealing with Max the lizard pointed to Garliva and her head was bagged by nearby dragons. The voice went silent. It was her. She was giving him pointers from the sideline.

Kicking max square in the chest he flew backwards towards the edge of the ring. His head landed next to the staffs that were stabbed in the ground. Before he could react the Lizard leapt at him pulling one of the staves stabbing Max in his arm. Max cried out to the top of his longes as the lizard grind twisting and pulling it around side to side to increase the pain. The dragon grabbed for another one and jumped up as to deliver a final blow directly to his head only to have Max grab the staff piercing his arm and yanked it in the direction of the dragon causing the dragon to be skewered through the middle of his body as he came down. The dragon lost grip as his body slid down the staff and exiting out the back of his shoulder. The final breath left the dragon with an eerie kind of gurgle. The sudden silence spoke volumes as the dragon leader walked up to him looking down upon his tiny body. Reaching down the leader pulled the dead dragon off the staff and passed him to a group of dragons as they carried him off in an almost honored way. With his free hand he took Max into it and brought him face to face.

"You are a clever and skilled warrior. Allowing yourself to be injured as to lure your enemy in with false hope then striking at the perfect time. You have proved yourself. You are now my Brood Brother. You shall stay at my side always along with your hatchery mate," the dragon said as Garliva was unbagged. Placing Max back on the ground the dragon smiled.

"Clean up my brood brother. He shall be honored with a feast," said the large dragon as he turned to his throne again once finished. The other dragons danced around Max making it hard for Garliva to even approach him. His look was the other reason. Max was still upset for some reason and she could not figure why. She did not get enough time bonded to him earlier to read his thoughts. It would either take another attempt, or she would have to try the old fashion way. Ask. Never the less both methods would require patients as neither were possible at the moment for the dragons where patching up his arm with dragon scales and leather wraps.

That night all of the village were gathered around a large bon fire cooking something that was smelling good. The female dragons danced around the fire as if they were belly dancers, but something they wore struck Max odd. Where those breast? A quick glance at one dragon that dropped one of the spherical objects off of her body only to quickly snatch it up and tuck it under a bra like leather garment gave him his answer. Garliva was having a great impact on these creatures. Garliva on the other hand was not enjoying the show as much as Max. She was possibly the furthest away from Max than anyone. She signed in frustration. Her plans might be on hold for longer than she would like. Suddenly a huge commotion echoed from the fire as the dragons that had been cooking danced up with a large golden platter with something meat related cooked and presented upon it. Stopping before Max they knelt down waiting for him. Looking up to the Larger dragon uncertain as what to do Max was presented a sharp object like a knife. They wanted him to sample the meat.

"Please as my brood brother you eat first in your honor," said the larger dragon. Reaching out with his good arm he sliced off a piece of meat skin and all. The skin sizzled and popped as it curled up rolling off the meat. Bringing the meat to his lips he found it carried an aroma that was unbelievable. Nipping a bit from it he found nipping was not going to be enough as he had to take a full on bite so he could rip and gnaw away at it. Finally he cut it free with his teeth he chewed it with each bite releasing wonderful flavor that made the almost jerky like toughness bearable.

"Mmm this is good," Max said nodding his head and presenting the meat in the air. Standing the larger dragon raised his arms above his head for all to see. The entire place went silent.

"My old brood brother has fought well, and died well. He now provides nourishment to my new brood brother. This honors them both. Take of him and eat well, he feeds us all tonight," said the dragon as the plate was carted away by the dragons as the dancing and singing continued. Max's eyes went wide. The creature he pulled meat from had fought him just hours ago and now the entire village would eat of his carcass. Garliva was the only one not taking of the meat. Her eyes fixed on Max.

The sun had gone below the horizon and the celebration came to a stop. All but a few had already gone to sleep for the evening. Kneeling down to max the larger dragon spoke to him directly.

"That was my former brood brother's cassic. It and all that is within its walls is yours," the dragon said before standing up to walk behind his throne. Oddly enough the dragon disappeared. Perhaps he simply slept behind the throne. But that was not what interest him as now he had a home. Not to mention what else his home had as well. Walking into the dwelling made of harden earth he was met by a dome like interior with vent holes that trailed up the ceiling. almost taking up most of the room was a round structure like a bed in the near middle covered in hides. It looked soft enough.

What caught him off guard was the small group of seven of the dancing dragon women posed around the bed smiling at him. Well as close of a smile that a lizard could produce. Seemed that being used as a social latter was happening quickly. All the dragons that were in his home wanted to be owned by the brood brother of the larger dragon. Possibly the highest honor one could have other than being owned by the larger dragon himself. How would that work? Considering how big the larger dragon was he could never produce offspring with any of the dragons in the village without killing them. Does he eat them instead? Kind of like a dragons having a sexy snack? I mean the dragons were not actually sexy by any means to a human, but who's to say how dragons pair off more or less do with a female of their own kind.

"We hope you don't mind but we would like to belong to you," one of the dragons said. Yep just as originally thought an honor to be owned by the brood brother.

"Yes we get so cold at night and you have so much warmth to give we figured you wouldn't mind sharing it with us," said another. Okay maybe not so much as an honor to be owned by, but to be warm. Sounded kind of bizarre, but he would have to go with it for now.

"Yeah whatever," Max was not in the mood to wonder or even guess the complex workings of the dragon society. For now he would just go with it and deal with the details tomorrow. As he was stepping upon the bed the lady dragons crawled on their knees towards him. Some of them quite large compared to him, others much smaller. As he laid down there was a few slaps exchanged by the dragons to jockey for position around Max but in the end they stopped. Throwing back the curtains of the place Garliva was about to speak when she saw Max look up at her covered in dragons. Garliva's first response was shock but quickly composed herself because she had to get close to Max at least to keep himself. Something was wrong with this group and she knew it. Closing her mouth she eased over to Max to have the dragons hiss at her.

"You stay at the feet. You have to earn the brood brother's grace," said one of the dragons clutching onto his arm exposing only his hand from her side. Conceding she dropped to her knees and curled up next to his legs. The dragons shifted around a bit before all were settled. Max laid his head back down upon the hides. Surprisingly enough they were very comfortable. The only thing that really bothered him was the fact that all the dragons around him had very cold skin. it was almost like they were sucking off his warmth. Thankfully it wasn't that cold out. Suddenly there was something furry and round that met his hand. Opening his eyes he didn't move a muscle. Giving a gentle squeeze it was soft yet firm. Probably Garliva's thigh or something. Either way he would just leave it be, and likely she would move from contact with his hand soon enough.

"Nou gab' my chest," Garliva demanded sitting right up growling at the dragon to her back.

"Sor-..." Max started when the dragon to her back sat up.

"You have warmth and we need it. So deal with it," hissed the dragon. Garliva rolled over towards Max pushing and shoving the dragons free of Max's body gaining all kinds of hiss and growls from them. Scooting until she laid next to max she laid stomach down next to him with his arm under her head. Just as quick as Garliva had forced her way to max the dragons covered the two leaving only their heads uncovered. From that moment on no one could move and no one did move.

The next morning Max woke to Garliva drooling upon his shoulder as her snores came off as brief and soft purrs. As amusing as it was her breath was not the most pleasant. In fact if he was not looking at her in the fact he would have swore he was next to a fish shop, with very old fish. Pulling his arm out from under her she stirred as she smacked her lips a bit wiping the drool from her face. Rolling to the side of the bed he scooted until he stood on the ground. Garliva suddenly sprung to all fours. Here eyes wide she forgot her goal and ended up falling asleep. Looking over at him she wondered if she would even have another chance. Dropping back on the bed planting her face in the furs she groaned to herself in frustration.

"Stretching Max started for the door when he noticed the dragons that slept there had dropped down a member or two but the ones that were still there were assisting each other in something that struck him odd. Before he knew it the two missing dragons came back with some kind of jelly like substance in several colors. Perhaps this was breakfast for them. Which this thought soon passed his mind as he watched the dragons make inceptions on the side of their ribs and slide the jellies into the openings. There was no blood and they did not even make a sound as they did this to each other. One by one they picked out the size they liked and for a lack of a better term implanted these orbs below their skin. Glancing over at Garliva who was now laying on her back they adjusted their orbs until they matched what Garliva had. Then they placed a jell on the out side upon the skin. Wrapping it in a leather like strap they finished it off by making sure the orbs could not move. It was creepy by all means but at the same time laughable. Mainly because the taller ones had the smallest orbs and the shorter ones had orbs that you would swore were implants. Technically they were implants.

Garliva was having an impact on the culture at least in his dwelling. Shaking his head he exited his new home to find almost all of the dragon females had done the same thing. As far as the eye could see they were wrapped with the same leather straps and chest filled with the jelly orbs.

"On the morning my brood brother," called the larger dragon with what was a clear smile far easier to tell compared to any other smile he had seen on the dragons.

"Good morning, uh...what is going on?" Max said pointing to a female dragon passing by with the new augmentation.

"Good...morning....yes that is a pleasant thing to say indeed. As for the latest, your hatchery mate has shown us a new liking. Soft egg shapes upon once ribs. According to your brood you had a fondness for them, causing your hatchery mate to grumble quite pleasantly," the larger dragon commented as it finally drew his attention. The dragons were all imitating Garliva's purr. Does that mean he was touching Garliva inappropriately all night? Suddenly Garliva stumbled out from the home bumping into Max's back.

"So'rry," Garliva stated placing a hand on Max's arm to steady herself while she still stared at the doorway.

"Seems we, or more to the point I have something in my sleep I ned to apologize for," Max started to blush. The larger dragon leaned down focusing on Max's cheeks.

"That is amazing. You have the ability to change the color of your skin," the dragon pointed out. Max blushed even more only to the delight of the larger dragon.

"Nou you nou touch me. I sing in sleep. Nou touch me on'any," She said. It could be seen that even her words were shaken a bit.

"What?" Max called back furthering his blush.

"You did not touch me at all. In fact only once or twice one of those lizards touched me and I pushed them away. I was purring because I was having a good dream not because someone was touching me," Garliva said directly into his mind.

"Then where did they get this idea from?" Max responded back to her mind. Wondering himself Max turned back to his door to peak in to watch the dragons of his, cup push and pull the orbs around working at perfecting their position within their bodies.

"What happened this morning while I was asleep," Max asked the tallest one.

"Szallsilic was asked what it was like to lay with the brood brother. She told them the story of the purring and told of a touch causing it,"

"Yes, Klmakila speaks the truth. I told them you touched..." the dragon started only to be interrupted by Max.

"Yes I know her breast. But why...what reason does every female here have these...balls of goo they are putting into their chests?" Max's words caught the attention of half of his group. Pulling him in Szallsilic kneeled down almost worried look upon her face.

"Please don't tell of our deception we would be devoured by our lord if he knew," she pleaded. The others huddled in close around the two same look of worry written in their gaze.

"All of your brood would be devoured for my mistake. I didn't mean to talk other then truth but I knew not what to say. I've never been brood of the brood brother," Said Klmakila as the others agreed with her. Even on her knees the larger female dragon had her chest in his face. Normally this was something he could have dreamt about but this. This was something more of nightmares.

"Okay okay, I'm not going to tell of your lie, but why did you started this fake...ball things?" Max was trying to address the subject without it getting strange. Not that it had not already. Klmakila spoke up first.

"Well not even moments after I had the tell, another's brood ran off to place brood nectar into her chest," she explained.

"Yes, this is true I was with her when it happened. While our bodies make nectar to survive the harsher winters and summers we do not make the amount we would need," Szallsilic only to have another pipe in as well.

"We gathered enough brood nectar for us by giving tells of our warmth with you."

"I had to let them touch of my skin," Commented yet another.

"What? why?" Max asked baffled as he stepped into the dwelling.

"So they could feel the warmth for themselves," the dragon did as close to a blush as possible as she lowered her head almost in shame. The other dragons around him did the same.

"Brood brother," called the larger dragon outside his home. Max leaned back to peak outside his door to see the leg of the larger dragon face to face.

"Uh yes I'll be right with you," quickly he closed the door again only to give them a quick message, "Keep this all to yourself. We will talk about this later." Stepping out of the door the larger dragon lifted him off the ground. Placing max on his shoulders the larger dragon walked off leaving Garliva to watch in horror. What was the larger dragon going to do to Max? She would have to guess as with the hustle and bustle of the morning she would not be able to follow easily.

Max's journey did not causing him any concern. He knew how easy it would be for the large dragon to do away with him if he wanted to. And it was not that the dragon gave him any idea of security. No, it was more that Max was jaded. Didn't really care if he lived or died.

Looking to his arm he marveled at the dragon scales as they shined and shimmered in the morning light. The leather held them fast to his broken arm. So much so that he could not bend it at all. They may not have seen a human before but they mended his arm fairly well.

Coming to a slow the larger dragon walked up the incline to the lip of a volcano to stand at the rim. Stepping one foot at a time the large dragon eased into the lava until his shoulders met the rim where he propped his arms up on it. A dragon sized hot tub, Max thought to himself. Stepping of the dragons shoulder Max met solid ground where he turned around to look at the lava. It was mesmerizing. Almost transcendent even.

"I know what you are," The dragon commented. Max looked up at the dragon in surprise. "Oh yes, your people have been here once before. In a time when I was much younger and another dragon was in my place. I was still quite tall but I was trying so hard to make Brood Brother. My day came when the brood brother of the time had fought a stranger that claimed to be an elf. Strange word but we accepted it. That elf challenged the brood brother and killed him. Very much like you did to my brood brother. The difference between you and them is two things. First, as soon as that 'elf' had killed the brood brother he attacked our god. I acted quickly and killed him in kind. Our god made me his new brood brother before another elf killed him. Thus making me the new god," The dragon looked down at Max as his arm came over steaming from the lava as the claw pointed towards Max. "The second is those ears. Not to mention your smell. You are elf, this I know, but not the same kind."

"Human, actually," Max corrected.

"Ah human elf. Very well human elf. I have made you my brood brother so that you can protect me from your elf brotheren. With you around I will stay god longer, and perhaps have peace with your people," the dragon stated as he smiled with his genius as he leaned back to relax. Max made to speak when someone else spoke in his place.

"How unfortunate as he has no pull in elf affairs. In fact his being your brood brother has guaranteed your destruction," called the elf that had started it all. Raising his hand elves ran up to the rim on the opposite side of the large dragon beside the elvish leader. Pointing their bows at the dragon they poised to fire.

"Kick the lava out!" Max called to an already tense dragon. With out asking a question the dragon used his panic to kick in the lava causing a wave to wash over the elves. The elves all died instantly except the leader who had made a protective bubble over himself. His anger grew as he watched his soldiers writhe in pain around him. Looking back to his enemy the dragon and Max ran from the volcano as the dragon snatched up Max in his still very warm hand and spread his wings. Swooping into the sky the dragon was well out of range for any of the elves to do anything.

"Are you okay?" Max asked of the dragon who did not look happy. Looking down at Max he didn't say anything for the moment. It took only seconds to land back at the village as the large dragon landed hard and stomped over to his throne flopping down in it. Tossing Max several dragons caught him and held tight in shock.

"Take him and his brood mates. They will all share his fate," The dragon said as all the smaller dragons looked over at the dragons and cat that were his. Each one snatched up they were lined up before the large dragon and forced upon their knees. It was going to be an execution despite Max saving the dragons life. Max hung his head. To have lived this long to die by the hands of something he never believed existed along side a cat that should not be able to communicate and others that got caught up in his war. If you could call it a war.

"An dis how repay life be sav?" Garliva caught the attention of everyone, "Tu be zacked, you life. He save you yes?" Garliva was quickly gaged along with everyone in his party. Holding up his hand the larger dragon paused the event. Motioning over his mouth for her to be ungaged he spoke.

"He did save me, but the human elf did not protect me from their rage," the dragon leaned almost angry, "So why should I bother keeping any of you around?"

"Because I know how to defeat them," Max said as he finally fought free of his gag. Looking over at Max Garliva whisper into his mind.

"You owe me. Which I plan to collect tonight,"

"Can we think on this another time? Trying to keep our necks from being stretched," Max's thoughts shot back.

"How would you do that?" the dragon asked.

"I've seen your people inflict tremendous pain and received tremendous pain. If they can't tell if you're hurt they can't tell if they hurt you. Then if you use whatever fighting ability you have you can easily push them from your world forever. Like...like the lava! Your people can hold the lava right?"

"Actually only a few. Most do not last long with it," The dragon answered back.

"Okay well a few is better then none. You saw how that elf had to struggle to save himself from burning while the others were crispy in seconds. Use the lava to your advantage. They cant touch it and you can. Hell make a mote around your village to protect you. Build up walls do whatever it takes to protect your people and yourself," Max instructed. No one moved or made a word for a time until the large dragon leaned down face to face with Max to snarl in his face.

"Fine! But if these ideas fail I eat you slow," the dragons hot breath felt like a blast furness as it hit Max's cheek.

"Use that too. Anyone gets too close to you blow your breath on them as hard as possible. They will turn away," Max explained. Everyone turned to the volcano as there could be heard the thundering march of troops headed their way. The large dragon stood up to take a look.

"We have but hours before they will be at our door steps. All of my children who can hold the lava gather up as much of it as you can. Those who dig well create a line around us in the ground to expose the lava. We will make a stand," The large dragon motioned for Max and his brood to be released as everyone got busy preparing for the fight to come. The dragons were so fast and accurate at their tasks they made ants look inefficient as they prepared. Max and Garliva helped where they could but were more in the way then anything else.

As the hour of war came upon them Max and all the dragons prepared for the worse as they watched intently to the horde of elves that formed around the village. Would it be drawn out, or would it be fast? No one knew. But it was clear the tension was so thick that fighting could break out any moment.

"I shall allow your people to live if you hand over the human and cat, Then kill your god," Called the elf leader. Max looked over his shoulders to see that none of the dragons even gave it a second thought. They were not going to kill the larger dragon, nor would they give up Max and Garliva.

"The human elf is my brood brother. You will not touch him....EVER!!!" yelled the dragon as his breath was expelled as hard as he could blow upon the Elves in the front row causing them all the near whither in the heat. Smiling in his sheer delight at the results he found a bout of confidence in the outcome of the war. It was short lived though as the leader elf Lifted his hand almost as if he was holding a cup in it and started to turn it over. As he did the ground beneath the dragons village shook and shook until it dropped sharply over and over again until finally all upon the ground in the dragon village found themselves falling into pitch black.

Chapter 11

Surreal

Max groaned as he lifted his head off the back of one of his dragons. Leaning up he found light dim but there. All around him there was light that peaked between the trees in the distance almost as if it was sunset all day, and never more than the equivalent of moon light was all they ever got.

"You still live?" asked Szallsilic as she aided him off the body he was resting on.

"Yes...Where is Garliva?" Max asked.

"She is here," called the distant voice of Klmakila. Seeing a figure walk towards Max and Szallsilic, he started to make out it was yet another of his dragons and slumped over her shoulders was Garliva. She was out cold but looked uninjured. The groans of the large dragon met their ears as his large hand nearly missed them as it passed over.

"What did they do to us human elf?"

"Seems he is the reason I was on your world in the first place," Max said as he reached over to Garliva as his hand and her body began to glow bright to his touch. All around them were large insects. They were not trees after all but the long legs of bugs. no sooner that they could see the creatures the creatures began to attack. Not even needing to be told Max and his entire brood were up and fighting to survive the insects that were snatching up those that were either dead because the large dragon had squashed them, or had not woken up yet and began to eat them. The large dragon blew his breath again this time it came out as an intense flame that ran off the ones in his path. Turning and blowing over and over he ran most of them off. Dropping to prop himself up with his arms he breathed heavy as he wasn't used to blowing fire that often or much.

"We need to move. Girls, help your god get to a safe distance, I'm going to see if I can find another way to run them off," Max ordered. He himself taking Garliva from the dragon to slump over his back like he had when they first met. The glow dimmed but did not go away. Following behind them Max frantically looked around for a solution to his problem. What would he do? They could hardly see the creatures and to add to it the world around them was very dark. Even if he could find something to do how would he know what he was actually doing? This was questions he would have to face. All around him he could see no solution. Looking back to the dragons that were trying to hurry away, they were pursued by the creatures of the dark place. Catching his own eye with the faint glow that was growing even dimmer Max thought to himself, she is the only way. We will have to come together again to save us all. Kneeling down Max started to lay Garliva on the ground when a blinding light beamed over his shoulder and a large limb like leg fell with a loud thud. The sound was almost as if a tree fell. Over and over again the beam of light cut the creatures to bits until they finally all just ran. Before too long the trees he thought he saw in the distance was gone and all that could be seen was the light that was barely there. Some one or something had just saved them.

From behind him came a light that was getting brighter until it was as bright as a lamp. Looking up he saw a haggard face. Old and leathery the person was almost human but looked like stone. Was it a human? Surely it could not be a human. Who, or whatever this was he would soon find out.

"So you are the new savior. And I see she is the new bond to tie you," the person said with a clearly old woman's voice. "You may want to follow me. We have much to talk about." Max was unsure to what to think of this 'lady', if that was truly what she was, as she seemed harmless enough. But as he had learned early on, nothing has been as it seems since he left his home. Standing back up and shifting Garliva on his back to better carry her, he followed the old woman. Her cloak glowed along the edges with interesting patterns. The flat surface began to wave as they traveled. They were crossing hills and small valleys that only insects would find massive but still it showed the land did have the possibility for change. As they started to climb an incline Max noticed there was almost a hazy pitch black layer they broke free as the air began to smell fresh and clean. Above the black layer there were stars above and hills that peaked barely above the black fog layer every so often. It was almost eery sight. Was this planet dead? More importantly why would anything other than that person that helped them even live on such a place.

"Come in my child. It is time you learn what you are, and what she means to who you are," the old lady explained as she opened the door to her old house.

It was a modest home on the outside nothing more then broken shutters and tiled roof that was missing a few here and there. Boards on the outside of the home were as old and gray as the ones on the inside. But within the walls he found to be more of a shock as there was a large chair for someone almost twice his size and one for the size larger of the old woman. Scattered about where things old enough to have been from his world's historical past.

"Please sit and I will get the tea," she ordered as she pointed to a chair she pulled from another room. Oddly enough the chair was large enough for Max to sit down Garliva and be able to sit next to her. Placing Garliva down first he sat beside her and waited for the old lady to return. Before too long she had returned with a cup of tea on a small platter and passed one to him and sat down placing the other on a table next to herself in the smaller of the two chairs.

"Who are you?" Max finally spoke. The old lady halted blowing on her tea and placed it down on the table once more.

"I am as you are. One of them," she explained which to him explained nothing.

"No, seriously who are you?" Max asked again.

"The vassal, just as she is. One intended to old the catalyst, which will bring balance and order back to all of existence. And like I was with my catalyst, you are bound for life. No other shall share nor tear your bond apart," smiled the old lady as she knew it would threw him for a loop.

"How is that...That doesn't make sense," Max retorted.

"Perhaps, but as I too was once of earth and under my king I found my king was not the only power in the land. Not only within my own land but in lands of others. Your world has been through this before. Our world has," she explained. But how was she still alive if she is talking about kings. The way she talked she was from the times of knights and kings.

"There is no way you could be from that time," he said.

"Oh? has that much time have passed to have become a world apart? Hmm, interesting. Not surprising as I was giving the gift of life long lasting by my catalyst. A gift I wish I was only able to share with him in kind." Tilting his head Max finally had to ask.

"Where were you from?" Max's words did not do anything at first as she slowly stood and looked out her window across the dark vail.

"I came to be in a time when knights were not something a woman could be. Punishable by death. Yet I found a dragon wise in time and age. I would slay him and take my place beside the other knights, and no one would be the wiser. That plan did not go well as that dragon was the catalyst. My contact with him bound his soul to mine and I became the vassal. Oh I was angry to be with such a foul beast. Over time I found a fondness for him and we finally became more then bound by soul but fight together as one. When our souls would combine we could take on any threat and become almost unstoppable," the old lady paused in her words as she turned from the window.

"See, this bond can only be broken when one dies. The other gains immortality instantly. A life where the body ages endlessly, but can never died as long as you do as the body needs. Eat...Sleep...Stay active," Her words trailed off as she walked back to her seat. Propping her hands upon her chin she smiled his direction.

"She is more important to you than you know. For if she lives along side you, you can keep you both alive. Once you die both will age,"

"Wait you said that when one dies the other gains immortality," Max interrupted.

"Yes, but you both have it and youth as long as the catalyst lives," She explained as max paused mouth gaping wide.

"Why did yours die?" Max really didn't want to know but yet at the same time curiosity was too much for him to stop. Probably something he gained from Garliva.

"To save me from being killed by his own people. You see the catalyst is always pulled from the people who need change. From that world comes the catalyst to create a better people upon it. The Vassal comes from a world that holds the answer to their change," she explained as she became visibly tired. Leaning back she blinked slowly a few times over and over.

"What's happening?" Max asked confused as to why she was drifting away.

"I have not maintained myself long enough that I can finally die. I grow tired of immortality and its endless loneliness.

Know that you must keep her safe at all cost. For if you die she gets immortality. If she dies you shall fade with her," The old ladies eyes grew heavy as she spoke her last words. "Even in death the catalyst lives on in the vassal...they...live...ooooooon." With that the lady moved no more. Her lifeless body a testament to her chosen mortality.

There was so much he wanted to ask her about what was happening to him but seemed he would not get the chance. Sighing deeply he stood up and walked over to her. Looking around the old lady he found a coffee table next to her with a book propped up against its side. Kneeling down he lifted it up into his hends. It was huge. Heavier than anything he had read before. Turning back around and grabbed his tea. Walking through the doorway between the two chairs he found a quant little kitchen with a small table set with an oversized chair and what he could only assume was the old ladies chair. Sitting in the old ladies chair he opened the books pages. The binding creaked as he turned over the cover. The pages were bound with the stitching of thread you would find in clothing. The pages seemed almost as reflective as gold. Each page showed drawings of her and the dragon. Those at the beginning of the book displayed the lack of skill in drawing, but as they went on it was clear she had plenty of time to prefect her art. The dragon in the image looked a lot like the dragons in which he was the brood brother of the leader, or god as they refer to him. Tall as two humans over the old lady. The images of her were impressive as well as she had long flowing blonde hair. Or was it red? It was hard to tell due to the lighting in the room but it was clear by the images they were at odds with each other for a long time. Then something changed. In the book it showed something tragic happening, not that Max could read it as it was almost abstract from the emotion in paint. Turning the page slowly Max was about to see what it was when he heard the the boards under someone's feet. Turning back around quickly Max was greeted to a sleepy Garliva rubbing her eyes.

"Where are we?" she asked. Max stood right up to stand inches from her face looking her in the eyes. She thought he would weep when his arms snatched her up in an embrace. His joy to see her okay was overwhelming even for her.

"What is wrong?" she asked curiously.

"Nothing," he said placing her back on the ground. Just then the ground around the house began to shake and Max fell over onto Garliva as the used the doorway to stop their fall.

"What was that?" Max asked as he scrambled back up lifting Garliva with him. Running to the front door he threw it open to be flooded with light. As his eyes adjusted they went wide and he quickly slammed the door shut.

"What? what was it?" Garliva asked. Jumping off of the door he took her hand and headed for the kitchen.

"It's time to go!" Max cried as he dragged her along through the kitchen as the house was bursting apart behind them. Not looking back Max backed in to the back door and slammed it with his shoulder thrusting right through it and rolling on the ground to a stop. Garliva colliding with him. Turning back the both of them darted separate ways as the beast that had just destroyed the house was still charging. Rolling to his knees he had little time to move again as Max about to be trampled by the oncoming hordes of creatures mowed everything down in they're way. Finally out of the way of the charging army of beasts he looked to where they were going to see another group of equal mass charging towards them as well. A darken circle surrounded what was left of the house. Seems they had been pulled and put into a new dimension again. Which was growing ever so tiresome for sure. When it finally struck him, where was Garliva? Frantically he looked around the other side to find she was not there. Even though the fight had reached back to where max was he bobbed and weaved through the struggle to get to the other side to see if he could find her only to find nothing. Not hide nor hair of his cat companion. With nothing more he could do he headed for high ground praying she had not been drawn into the fray.

Chapter 12

Awaiting

It had been months since he had arrived in this new place. Garliva had not been seen by his eyes for more time than he would like to admit and for a time he grew ever so skeptical he would ever see her again. A brief had started at him this very morning. Something that had not been done before. Each time he felt the pain it felt as if he was in another body. More to the point her body. Garliva. Chalking it up as missing her more than anything he went on. For this day he would start his first day as his new job. A job he was not sure if he was ready for, but had no choice as he was hungry and the local ruler would only feed him if he would fight in his arena. Seemed no one would due to how dangerous it was. If he had thought a bit clearer he could have started a farm on land somewhere and had not needed anyone to survive. With Garliva gone he could not think clear again.

Walking through the arch way he approached a man on a thrown that looked more like the devil to him then an actual ruler. Red in skin tone he sat regally upon his golden thrown. Standing he wore a tunic like that of the romans with gold lace that trailed the bottom in an interknit pattern. Max paid it no mind as he had to make a deal with the devil as he saw it. Upon the red skinned rulers head was a crown of sorts that looked more like leafage that curled upwards around his horns. Being of a religious background he could only think of the elder members that would have scoffed at this sight if not try to burn him at the stake with their torches and pitchforks.

"Ah Hiltitus, You have made it," said the ruler to Max. Again he had given a fictitious name to conceal his identity. Bowing his head in respect Max made sure to follow what he had seen others do when standing before the ruler.

"Today we shall start up out slow. You shall face a boar in front of my people. It's a rather large boar so don't think it will be as simple as it sounds. Now, follow Thigdenion. He shall arm you," said the ruler as he waved Max away. Following the daemon like figure covered in roman attire Max was drawn deeper and deeper into the building until he came to a room where the walls were covered in weapons of both old and new. Many which did not look as if they belong in the time period that the world projected to be in.

"You may pick of any bladed weapons, and armor only of metal," Thigdenion instructed before he turned and walked away. The door slammed behind him and the sound of a lock holding in place.

"Seems like there is no turning back now," he muttered to himself. Looking over the blades and various forms of armor Max could feel sharp pains that were seemingly come from nowhere. He would have to fight through them as he was hungry and the only way to eat was to fight, and kill this boar.

Without removing his own attire Max adorn himself in light armor and a sword and small more like oversized gauntlet, yet it was a shield.

"It is time. Follow me," Said Thigdenion. Turning the rubbing of metal could be heard from his armor as he moved. Being led down another long hall and up a tunnel into a large roman like arena Max stood before a cheering crowd. He came off almost stoic as he turned to look around at all the cheering fans. Surely they were not there to cheer for him considering it was his first time to be in this place. Deciding that would come later he looked at the other door as it opened to black of nothing. The crowd gasped. Max turned to the ruler raising his arms only to be redirected back with a pointing gesture. Turning back just in time Max was able to lean forward and use the shield to absorb most of the blow. Rolling on the ground he was stunned to see a boar as large as he stood. They were dangerous enough without being large this one was more of a nightmare.

How would he survive this, he thought. The boar started charging him again. Over and over he dodged back and forth trying to find a weakness only to find none. Perhaps he would have to get the creature to charge and hit a pillar or something so it would daze it long enough to strike. Getting near one of the pillars he let the boar charge him. Just at the last moment he jumped out of the way to find the boar barreled right threw it causing the pillar to crumble. Now Max has something else to worry about as he had to dodge falling stone. Looking up he glanced down to find the boar had turned around and about to hit him at the same time when a stone landed on the boar's head rolling his way. Moving out of the way Max ran around the stone and struck the boar where the stone had made an opening. Effectively the boar was finally slain. Standing up the ruler and his people cheered loudly.

"My people, we now have a champion ready to slay the beast of Delvendor. We will place our champion against a few more opponents before we have the Delvendor beast for the final showdown. Rest well our champion, for you have slain our beast of the forest. You have deserved it," The ruler said as people came out taking away the boar. If he wasn't so focused on his next meal Max could have realized the inflection in his voice. This kingdom's ruler intended sinister plans that involved max.

That night they feasted and Max ate and partied waiting the dances of unclothed beings of whatever they were.

"Do they not please you my champion?" the ruler asked of him. Wiping his face with his arm in a most uncivilized way Max replied.

"They are fine," Max replied.

"Then perhaps you would prefer..." the ruler began only to interrupt his own words by clapping his hand causing the gender to change on the dancers. From sleek and sexy to thick and beefy. Normally this would have shocked him but at this rate he was starting to become num to it all. A fact that escaped him at the moment.

"Heh, okay," Max said turning back to his food. His true focus was still on Garliva. She may have been away from him but she had become a part of him and like loosing an arm or leg he felt uncomfortable, struggling even, without her. Keeping alive was important he thought to himself. This was the only reason he was not out there looking in the scorching hot desert combing it for her as he should. Besides it had been long enough that the only way she was still alive was if she had been captured. He still felt the pains and flashes of visions like he did when the humans were hurting her, so fur sure she had to be alive. It was the only hope he had left in him. Still, even that little bit was powerful enough that thinking about it for a brief moment was enough to revitalize his faith that he would see her again.

Nearly a year had passed and what was like a weekend of every week he would step into the arena to fight some ungodly creature. He had even managed to control the reflection of pain and torture he suffered from out of nowhere. Truly he had become the people's champion. Never mind that the fact that when he would walk by the people in the streets of the city it felt like they were mere puppets if nothing else. No sales transaction ever completed and no actual conversations. Just repeating actions and words. As if he was in a funhouse full of animatronics just following the same routine set day in, day out. He let the thought pass each time he wondered about it. This was not the time he thought. Keep his mind in the game as it was. After yet another creature slain he followed Thigdenion back to the same armory he suited up in for over a year. Of course calling it a year or the passing of a week, a week, was all assuming that their time was as our own. Still it worked in his mind.

"Another fight well done Hiltitus," said Thigdenion as he took each piece of armor and weaponry from Max. "Tomorrow you will face our greatest enemies champion and help decide the fate of two worlds. Ours the most just and noble of lands and that of Carnazoron land of evil and death. May you rest well till this day ends," said Thigdenion as he walked away leaving Max to his thoughts nodding in conformation. Of course that meant he would be the champion of the land and he would be able to go anywhere and be provided as decreed in his agreement with the ruler. Probably the worse thing to be thinking about when he had someone to find, but in his mind if she was still alive, and he was certain she was, it would be much easier to get co-operation from the people if he was the champion. Or at least that is what he thought. Heading to the small place he slept every night he kept his mind on the task at hand. One more day, he kept thinking to himself. Just one more night.

The next day had finally arrived. He would be ending one journey and starting another. Keeping his mind on task was harder then usual as he knew this was likely going to be one of the toughest battles he had ever fought in his life, or in his colosseum career. Dressed and waiting the morning was a blur the fear of what could be worse then that twenty foot tall beast he had faced not more than a week ago would be scary, but he did know how to best it faster. No this could not be so simple, surely it was even larger than that. These thoughts raced through his mind over and over as his anticipation rose. Walking through the tunnel he raised his arm with his sword just like he normally did stirring up the crowd. He would give them their greatest show they would ever see in their life. This would be beyond a doubt...then he paused mid thought.

Standing on the other side growling was something sounded familiar. It drew his entire attention away from his previous thought. Scraggly covered in blood and foaming from the mouth he saw the creature. So distorted there was no way it could be her, but he could feel it.

Something drew him towards her. Stepping one foot in front of another he tilted his head. This was a formidable beast alright but not what he expected. Was it truly her? Could it be? Loosing grip on his sword he dropped it to the ground as his eyes went wide. It was her. He had found her without having to go far. But where was she the whole time? How come she didn't come looking for him?

All that he would find out later, right now it was time to rejoice he found Garliva! Running to her he went to embrace her only to have her try to take off his head. Rolling to the ground he could see she was delirious and attacking. The fact was backed up by her coming at him with another volley of fur and claw. Nearly escaping her attack he sat back on his haunches. Touching upon his cheek he, it coated his finger in blood. What was he going to do? If he fought back she could get hurt. Considering he had just barely found her there was no way he was going to loose her again, even to his own hand. But at the same time if he did nothing she would kill him in no time. There was only one option he had left.

Dodging back and forth he struggled to get away from her. With each strike she got closer and closer to him. Running short on time as it wasn't too long before she would overwhelm him, he knew he needed something between him and her to change the rules of the engagement. Seeing a small pillar on the outside of the middle of he arena he dashed over in a full run after she lunged and missed him again. Knowing she was following he darted around the pillar with her behind him. Around the turn she loss her footing and fell. Completely running around the pillar lifting his sword. With one which motion he smacked her on the back of the head with the blunt side of his steel. Even with all his effort the blade did not hit exactly how he wanted. Nicking the back of her head he was met with a spray of red upon the wall. His heart nearly stopped thinking he could have did more damage than he had expected. Her body slumped over completely motionless. Dropping his sword he went to kneel beside her only to feel a massive rumble than the voice of his captor echo out.

"Did you think it would be so easy as that? This was not the final battle, it was merely a test to see which of you would face the final. Now let the real challenge begin."

The center of the arena lifted up higher and higher until from beneath the earth emerged a massive armored worm type creature tentacles. The dirt in the middle dropped suddenly and within the whole there of was massive teeth. These teeth were like jagged saw blades angled in all directions that would grind up anything that comes near them. Aligned all around the teeth were more tentacles that whipped around in all directions.

If his heart had not sunk before now there was a bigger problem. Thankfully being behind the pillar would help. Or at least he thought. No sooner did the thought cross his mind the pillar started falling his direction. Scooping her up in his arms he hugged her close as he knew with how much armor he, and her were wearing, not to mention her body weight as well, he knew he wasn't going far or fast from it's on coming impact. The ground shook but they were not flatter then before. Opening his eyes he saw that the pillar had hit the wall and fell behind them. Seems that luck was still on his side for the time being. At least until the ground started to sink towards the open mouth. Sliding towards a pending doom he held her closer to his body.

"Come on Garliva! I need you. I can't do this with out you!!!" he yelled closing his eyes as they streamed tears. Pressing his cheek to hers his consciousness faded away.

All was dark as pitch. He opened his eyes slowly to find they were back in the world of aura again. However this time she was not glowing like before and what aura was there was faint. The back of her head was darker red the he had ever seen before. Where her brain was, held a purplish green hue, almost like illness. Reaching up he caressed her head in his hands and placed his head to hers. The two auras blended into one.

"Hello? Anyone there?" He called out. There was no answer to his call. A short distance was a dime light that flickered in and out. Where was this? He thought. Surely this was not what the afterlife was. What was that in the light? Could it be the key to it all? The words in his head continued. Approaching slowly the figure under the light got clearer. It was Garliva, and yet it wasn't. Her same markings, colors and overall feel. But this one was different. Thin body, dis shambled fur and overall unkept.

The closer he got the more he noticed her body was emaciated and withered. As if she had starved for months. No emotions or even sign of life emanated from her as the light rained down upon her dimly. Reaching out he took hold of her arm to find his fingers wrapped completely around her feeling only bone. What had done this to her? what could have been so powerful to turn her this way so quickly? Was his thought until he realized he was also hearing her voice as well. It was so low that it came off as white noise. kneeling down he heard it clearer but her lips were not moving when it dawned on him that his words were not uttered either. Were these thoughts? If they were she was in a bad way as only words she was saying were about letting go of life and all her failures when a key word perked his interest.

"I have failed my mate. Max will never forgive me for my failures," he heard. Mate? She thought of him as a mate? This brought such joy out of him his body started to glow as if it was it's own light source. Wait, the thought caused a reaction? So what you thought in whatever world they were in would thank the very fabric of reality and perspective, and no thought could be hidden from the world.

If he held all these facts to be evidence of the truth then she loved him as much as he loved her. Loved her, he thought. Yes he did think it. Was this something that even he did not realize within himself? The last time they had connected it was nothing like this. Whatever this was it had taken them on a whole new and even more personal level. Then he thought back to the old lady that had mentioned having fall in love with a dragon. This must be the level of connection she had that could not be explained. Then the thought crossed his mind how she mentioned that one always out lives the other. Suddenly the light from him started turning blue to match his emotion. Reached over he pulled her to face him cupping her cheek with one hand. Her eyes stayed closed even to his touch. As he looked upon her, he studied every aspect of her face from one end to another and found it was true, his feelings were so strong for her that seeing her so near death formed a pit in his stomach that only grew with each moment he knew there was nothing he could do to help her.

"Garliva please wake. Don't leave me. I know life is harsh and the world is far from fair but..." he paused as a tear rolled down his face. "I can't imagine life without you anymore. I can't go on if you are not in it. I need you." With that he pressed his lips to hers softly sliding his cheek along. Lovingly he kissed her eye and cheek then placed his cheek to hers breaking into a full on cry. So this is how it ends he thought the light from him lowered to as dim as hers. He continued to hug her close. At least if he was going to give up he would not be alone.

Just then something in Garliva began to stir as her words stopped all together and her ear pivoted to the sound of his voice sobbing. Peering open she looked into space for a moment before her voice was heard.

"Love?" echoed from her. Before his eyes a light grew from her instead. As he leaned back to notice his light grew too. Her over all mass filled out and her face became more plush again. It was as if she was going back to normal before his eyes.

"I...do" She added looking him in the eyes. Smiling he stared right back. She was interacting with him again. This was a miracle!

"It is no miracle. It was you. You said..." She began as he piped in.

"Ah, right I forgot that thoughts cannot be hidden here." He blushed a bit as she cupped his cheek this time and her eyes began to well up.

"It's true then? What I heard was...Is" she said never loosing sight of his eyes. Nodding he closed his eyes laying his forehead to hers breathing a sigh of relief. Normally he would have pulled away and never said anything with the word 'love' in it. Not even to family. But she was different. She brought out something he had never felt before. Opening his eyes he looked down to see she was not wearing anything but he was. Seems he had more to hide than she did. Figured, considering she was far more open and forward with everything she said and did. Being the world he came from it was not uncommon for everyone to hide something.

"Well that was quite anticlimactic wasn't it? Thigdenion, Ready my..." The dictator began only to be interrupted by events in the arena.

Whatever was happening caused the creature that had been the main event now only a foot note as it screamed a horrible sound. It was clear it was in pain as the tentacles were bashing the walls and thrashing the crowd. Deep in the middle a myst of blood and tar clouded the view. Further and further out from the middle the flesh of the beast bubbled and boiled. From within the myst a bright light grew until it caused the myst to be blown away. With a deep guttural sound the creatures tentacles crashed down lifeless in the stands. From where the light glowed strongest a form could be made out. Around that form all the winds and myst flowed around in a vortex type sphere.

"You sought to destroy that which was to bring peace and life. You had succeeded before but never more. With this, your time ends for all time," called out the figure of light. As the light became more focused and it showed who it really amongst the winds. A creature of a perfect blind of human and cat. Not entirely male, not completely female. A being of both and of neither. One thing was for sure, the being was unmeasurably powerful and was about to rain down unholy destruction upon their tormentors.

Chapter 13

Return

Laid upon the ground panting heavily Max opened his eyes to a world scorched. The ground nearly turned to glass from the actions he and Garliva had done. Leaning up he could hear the cracking of glass beneath his hands. Small barbs and shares embedding in his flesh. Looking around there was nothing left standing. Only the sight of bright embers danced about. Effectively the arena was gone, as was everything else. Only thing that even show there was any structure at all was a few bricks, and the startings of walls that were charred pitch black. Moving to sit up he found he was being cut by the glass below him with each movement. The blood started to pool under him. However that was far from the focus of his concern. Quickly looking about he sought out his furry companion.

"Where was she?" he thought. Near in a panic he was placed at ease when his eyes gazed upon the orange of her fur as she too sat up. Her breathing labored as well. Releasing a sigh of relief his eyes met hers as she turned in her frantic search for him. What they should probably worry more about was how they were going to get out of the pit without cutting themselves up all over considering both of them were as bare as the day they were born. Not that it mattered considering she was so content to have him in her sight that her purr was echoing all over the crater. He could not help but feel at pease just simply at the sound of her purr.

******

Shaking of the ground set everyone off steady as they jockeyed for balance. Hurrying around Jabber grabbed the baby and Annabelle peering above for anything falling.

"It's okay baby's momma, I'll get you out of here safe," He ensured.

"I ain't this baby's momma you dolt," Annabelle shot back cradling the baby close. The baby cried. It was clear there was a great amount of irritation endured by the couple for sometime at how they reacted to the cry.

"Damn, can't you shut that baby up?" Jabber complained.

"Well if you had not lost the baby bag maybe we would have changed the baby's diaper by now and we would have peace and quiet," She shot back when she realized what she had done. Annabelle paused and began to apologize only to have Jabber about to start at the same time. again unable to finish as they were to start talking again the ground began to shake and then before them was a sudden crater before them and in the middle stood Max and Garliva. Clothed in practically nothing and covered in blood and shards of glass sticking out on their sides and hands.

"What tha?" Jabber uttered as he stood up recognizing Max right away. Running over to them Jabber took hold of max's arm to help him out only to pull his hand away looking down to the glass that had cut his hands.

"Dag, dog you got yourself all messed up. What happened to you?"

"Y'know I'm sure they are happy to see us as well but we bess get out of here before we are found," Annabelle interjected.

"Oh yeah she's right max, we got problems right now. We are being hunted. Makes me feel like back in the days when my people..." Jabber started.

"Don't! don't you dare being up the 1800s," Max said.

"What? my people suffered and we shouldn't for get that. Black Lives matter," he added only to be ignored as they headed for cover. "Well they did," Jabber added.

"You guys are a mess,"

"Heh i'm sure we feel worse than we look," Max said in response.

"That is for sure," Garliva nodded in agreement.

"Holy Shiz, meowmix talks. When did that happen?" Jabber asked.

"Remember when her and I would,...uh, start....glowing?" Max asked.

"Yeah," Jabber replied only to get a weird look from Annabelle. "Oh, don't worry about it boo I'll tell you about it later," He said dismissing her so he could listen to Max again.

"Okay well," Max began again as he started to sit down but hopped back up. The glass barbs made it impossible for him to sit. Without saying a word Garliva started helping him get the glass out of his skin. Flinching everyone in a while from the pain he explained, "Those times we glow we are...uhh." Garliva pipped in as she made eye contact with Max.

"Becoming one," she told them all.

"That's probably the best way to explain it. So my thoughts are her thoughts and her's are mine," No sooner he spoke those words that Jabber added his two cents.

"So like Mr. Spock? You know a mind meld."

"Yeah," was all Max said as he turned and started pulling glass from Garliva. Each of them pulling deeper and deeper in the skin of the other. Jabber making a face as if he was going to vomit.

"Oh cut it out," Annabelle commented bouncing the baby around a bit as she turned back to Max and Garliva.

"You guys look like you were used as a pin cushion." Max grimised to Garliva digging in his flesh to pull out the glass as it broke. Placing his hand on hers Max stopped Garliva's actions.

"I think there is an easier way," He informed her. Annabelle and Jabber glanced at each other.

"Yes. Not good time for yet," Garliva leaned over a rubbed her nose to Max's cheek before standing up and looking around. Then addressing Jabber and Annabelle she continued, "You hide like small...uhh," Her words stuck on a word she did not know.

"Mouse," Max added.

"Thank you," Garliva said before continuing, "Yes, mouse."

"Yeah well y'see," Jabber was about to explain when he and Annabelle dropped down lower to the screeching of something beyond the cars and brick walls. When it just hit them, this was Max's world. Everything was as if it was drawn out from different parts of cities on earth. In the middle of where Max and Garliva showed up was a spread of glass. Looking at each other the hair on both their necks began to raise. What it all meant was that if parts of his world and hers could be pulled into one existence then there was no telling what else was in the world with them. At their current state there was no way that Max and Garliva would be able to merge as they had before. There was way too much healing needed first.

The shadow of the object above drew their attention back to the situation. Glancing up to get a look was would not work as the sun was blaring too hard. The only reasonable choice was to find cover and regroup their efforts. Jumping up Garliva and Max both grabbed Jabber and Annabelle running for what was left of a building near by.

"Dag don't be grabbing me. You're going to be getting your body juices all over me," Jabber complained. Annabelle did as well but not a verbal.

Chapter 14

Final Chapter

Opening his eyes he was met with a dark room where barely any light came through. Something was in the room with him, but he could not make it out. Feeling no threat from who or what it was he reached out his hand to feel thick fur. The feeling was near bliss under his fingers as he closed his eyes feeling further into the fur. His hand stopped when he hit raises in the skin below the fur. Going up just a bit further it was clear his hand was groping the plentiful breast of some fur covered woman. His action was met with a growl as it was pushed away. It wasn't that aggressive so he leaned up to get a better look. There before him was a vixen. Clearly humanoid in shape. Her teeth were bared, and yet again he did not feel the hostility that should have accompanied it.

"Don't touch me," she growled.

"I'm ...not," he went to respond when it dawned on both of them they were both speaking the same language. This should have been strange as his mind made the logical argument, fur does not cover the body of a human, and yet it did not strike him as odd as it should have. Something strange was going on and he had no idea what it was. The only thing was clear is this creature was familiar to him. Turning away from her She did the same as they both looked around to find a fully furnished room and they were both under sheets upon a bed. Standing from the bed first he found he was bare.

Yet this was not what bothered him it was the fact that his dark skin seemed like it was out of place. Was he a black man? Walking up to the mirror over the dresser he peered upon himself to see his head was shaved close and his skin as dark as milk chocolate. She joined him at the mirror to find her ears pointed up ward and her muzzle was long and narrow.

If that was the case then way did she feel the fox like appearance didn't belong? Was she not a cat? A question they both shared as their minds were linked.

"Why am I covered in red fur?"

"Red fur? Why am I so dark?" He asked. Reaching out they both placed their hands upon each other's chest in the center. Flashes of visions broke through their minds but did not stay. Far too quickly flashing for them to grasp exactly what was happening they let go.

"I guess maybe all that was a dream,"

"And we just both have the same dream? I mean I don't even have my accent and I'm not talking directly into your mind," The vixen complained crossing her arms. Lifting his hands in a fully body shrug he stopped at the sight of gold around his ring finger. Drawing it in closer he was stopped as she took his hand and looked at it closer.

"Is that what I think it is?" She marveled at the ring of gold. However he did the same as she held his hand up he noticed she had one like his. Taking her hand in his he looked it over and over.

"We're married?" For him this was puzzling. For her it made her heart soar at the thought of what the ring meant. Pulling her hands from his she laid her body upon his and hugged him close. It was at that moment that they both realized they both smelled of a honeymoon.

This caused them both to blush.

"I best take a shower," he said.

"I'll join you," she replied. He wanted to refute it but he was already naked before her and covered in her smell, how much more worse could it get?

Just as they had planned they did indeed take a shower and each in turned helped wash the other's back. She still had those certain mannerisms that made her just like the leopard she could have sworn she was. He the same for his counterpart. Neither argued or discredited their current who they were, but said nothing about it.

As they got dressed they found weird memories of jobs and tasks they were suppose to do come to the for front of their mind. Where were they coming from? What was the purpose of having the other life if this was who they were all the time?

Dressed in a business suit it felt weird. For some reason it looked out of place even in his new body. Like he was suppose to have something as simple as just jeans and a shirt with a pair of work boots. Or overalls that were given to him by a farmer. Obviously he was not going to be able to figure this out right away so he tucked his keys for a car in his pocket and his money along side it, but when he picked up the phone he found it was cracked in a spider webbed pattern and a small dome like indention upon it's glass.

"Honey what tha hell did you do to my phone?!" He called as he rounded the corner where she was cooking small pieces of meat.

"I had to knock that arrow out of Jabber what do you want?" She said with a bit of attitude when they both turned pale. Jabber. They both know of him, but how would that be unless they were not in their own bodies.

"Something's not right," He said. Letting go of the pan she quickly grabbed his arm and hand.

"This is a trick. Someone is feeding us these images," she said as sure enough a clapping of hands came from behind them. There stood the elf that started it all.

"So you have found each other. I should have known it was you two from the first moment I laid eyes upon you. You certainly peeled apart my dream state for you,"

"What do you want?"

"To remove all filth from all dimensions for ever. You hinder my peoples ability to rule, and thrive and I won't have it anymore. So with that You may die now," He elf said as she raised his hand to destroy them only to find he was blocked by Max stepping hi front of Her to block her from the blast.

"Leonard! NO!" She said wrapping her arms around him and pressing her face to his back closing her eyes. Like an inferno's blast their flesh was peeled away like the ash from a fire and they were left in a dark.

Slowly a faint glow emanated from two very close sources. As they glowed brighter they outlined his and her original bodies. Loosening up he turned towards her as she never took her hands off his sides. His hands found her arms as their auras were both covered in the tiniest small red stars that twinkled so brightly. Neither spoke a word but their emotions spoke volumes. The feeling of love for one another lit up the whole world as all that around them burst into light. The beauty of it all was overwhelming, even though they did not partake of thing other than each other.

"I feared loving you, for fear of judgement and shame. As shame that was unjustified. I see that now and no matter what judgement may befall me I want to love you and cherish you for as long as time will permit,"

"I may have had no shame, and focused on anger when I met you. You look like that which has destroyed my people for many of times passed, but you are not. You are my heart, my soul, and I live not, if I am without you," Garliva said answering Max.

"And that is the secret that I was never able to find in my time," said the old woman. Both Max and Garliva turned towards her to find a massive dragon standing beside her. Smiling she continued, "My ignorance had blinded me from everything that we had accomplished," she reached up to take the finger of her dragon counter part.

"Our species may be world apart just like yours, but that does not mean they have to stay apart. Be the beacon of hope and truth for all worlds to see," With that the old woman and dragon's forms came together and in a brilliant show of light faded off like smoke blowing away in the wind. Looking back at each other they both glowed as the small red starts started to flow from their from and encircle them like a cyclone. As the two inched closer to one another the storm of red grew bigger and bigger as they glowed brighter until their lips pet and all was so bright it was all that could be seen.

Pulling from her, Max noticed he was kissing Garliva and her eyes were streaming tears just as his was. Both of their bodies were freed of all the shards of glass. All around them was a cleared area like the cyclone of glass had cleared it out for them. Looking up they found the elf their angered at them breaking his deception. As they stood the elf was about to attack again when from the side his herm of dragon females started smacking the elf with sticks and other objects while the dragon god came in smashing everything in his path to try and kill the elf. Joining the fight glass wolves of green grabbed the elf's arms and ripped at them, followed by the shotgun sound of the officer that had too became glass.

"Hope you guys are planning on helping, my boys and I can't hold him off forever," The officer explained as the sounds of the glass shattering along with the eerie glass wolves screams of pain came from all around them. Collecting what wolves he had left, the officer ordered them away while firing his shotgun at the elf. Each shot found an invisible force deflecting his shots.

"I think we best get dress quick and get into this fight. No sooner that he said that his dragon females came up to them both and helped them dress in the dragon tribe attire. Bowing they kneeled before him.

"Brood Brother we have come to aid you," Szallsilic said as she lifted a odd looking primitive like blade up to him.

"Go aid our god in your quest to balance the world," Klmakila added. No sooner that they did all the female dragons ran off except Szallsilic. She walked over to Garliva and placed her hand on the cat's shoulder.

"I am honored to be the brood brother's mate under you," she said before joining her fellow lizards. Looking over at each other they admired each other for a moment.

"You look pretty hot in anything you wear you know that?" Max commented

"I was just thinking the same," She said, her accent had all but left her words. They had touched each other so closely they were able to aid each other without even trying.

Just as they turned to join the fight both Max and Garliva dodged the large dragon flying past them and smashing through a wall. As much as the elf may have not been as large as the dragon he wielded more power than all of them put to gather. However it had taken a toll on the elf's body as he was showing clear signs of fatigue. Dropping down low to slide next to the elf's legs he sliced off the elf's leg just below the knee while Garliva cut off his hand he was using to attack them. Falling flat he hit with a thud for but a moment until he levitated above the ground. The air around him grew darker as a red aura started to form.

It was in that moment it was clear, he was a vessel for something as well.

"He's the destroyer," both Max and Garliva uttered out as the hair on the back of their next stood on end.

"Tha what?" Jabber said as he came up behind them to stand next to one of the taller female dragons. His eyes looking over the uncovered bosom of the dragon only to be smacked by Annabelle.

"Sorry boo, they are just so big...and juicy looking," Again Jabber was smacked. "Why you gotta go an do that?" He cried.

"Cause you attckin' a fool,"

"I'm sorry boo," was all he could say. The dragon puffed out her chest with pride. These brood nectar's were attracting those like the brood brother, and this was greatly pleasing to her.

"Because Jabber, we are the bringers of peace, he is the bringer of death,"

"Correction. I killed death and in doing so I gained all his powers," the elf said as his leg and hand grew back in a blackish red tar like material and solidified before their eyes. No sooner that his new limbs were formed a large car was tossed at the elf knocking him a distance away. The large dragon had gotten back to his feet and threw it at him.

"Oh thank god you are okay,"

"Yes my brood brother. You honor me,"

"Not as much as you honor me. Now I need you do something for me. Save all your people and any of my people by getting them out of here and protect them with your life,"

"As you wish my brood brother," The large dragon graved the humans from behind Max and with the female dragons they ran for safety. The glass wolves right on queue followed the dragons away from the scene. Looking over to them the officer saluted them before he too ran off.

"Lets who him the power of our love," Garliva said as she stood beside him facing the elf.

"Wow that sounds so corny, but right now it's the only way to put it. Lets to it!" Max started to glow as did Garliva and neither of them touched one another. Their bond was now so strong that they were able to reach the celestial planes in reality without making contact. Both of their bodies grew in size and started to match the shape of the being they turned into when they had merged before. As they talked both voices of Garliva and Max were heard as if they were talking at once with a powerful echo.

"You found power only threw you're hate, and that hate is limited to the object there of. It has no chance of beating what we have formed. Therefor, you must be no more so that life can thrive again, in love," they said to the elf. As they watched the elf had the sounds of braking bones and ripping skin as his body contorted into something a kind to a dragon but more like a demon. He was now twice their size.

"You spout all of your riotousness as if it's the only truth. When even you don't believe in that power, wouldn't you say Icaas?"

Max just stood there as neither of them moved.

"Would she still love you if she knew what you did? The wrong you can never atone for? The life you sacrificed for the sake of anger, Johnny?"

"Max don't listen to him, He's trying to break you down," Garliva was trying to calm him in his mind as she spoke directly to him.

"Or would you kill her too, just as you did...your wife and child?" Max fell out of the glowing form and back to his human form. Panic clear upon his face. The demon elf had struck a nerve. Falling out of her form too Garliva caught Max. He looked up at her before pushing away.

"He's right. I did kill them. I don't deserve you," he said as he started to cry before her.

The laugh of the demon could be heard from far and wide as he stepped closer. Cupping her hands around his face she pulled his nose to hers.

"Leonard I know..." she started when his whole body calmed and his eyes locked with hers. In that moment we went back to the memory.

On the day, he was riding along in his car with his wife in the passenger seat while his child was strapped in behind them. While the details were not as clear as they should have been, he could remember the last second decision to swerve, and right in to a truck turning over the car and pinning them all against trees off the side of the road. A decision made in anger as him and his wife had argued just before. What he could not recall. It was that argument and the fact he could not remember it that he felt he was the reason for their death and would not forgive himself for it.

Drawing him back out of his thoughts Garliva cupped his cheeks.

"I know what you did, and I forgive you," she said just as the sound of the demon's mighty claw sliced into her chest from the side. Her face went blank as her body slid off his claw and on to the ground.

"Ha ha ha, you will roam this world forever alone and ever aging filth human," the demon elf said.

"she was the vessel, I was the catalyst," he said. The demon's eyes went wide as he knew he had killed the wrong one. The truth was as long as the Catalyst still lived both could live as long as he could sustain her body before she died. If he was not able to then they would both die. Swinging quickly to try and cut Max down the demon elf missed. Dropping to his knees he scooped up her lifeless body as he could still feel the warmth that was fading from her. He had little time. Cupping her cheeks he held her face firmly as he drew his lips to hers and everything around them melted away. They were back in the celestial plane. But this time everything was quickly fading to black. Her body was there and the black void was working its way up her chest when he quickly jabbed his hand into the celestial form of her body right where the black void met. He screamed out in pain. Taking hold of the void he could feel his arm turning red as it did when he snuffed out the red stars of body before, but this time it was worse. With his free hand he took the stars from where his hard lay and pulled half of them out. Opening his hand the glow of the stars were bright. While holding back the void he added to her heart his stars.

At first nothing happened. Half her body was missing as it was completely blanked out as if it did not exist below the void, but what he had failed to realize was he was the whole reason they both existed in the first place. Without him they would never have been able to save the worlds. Or her.

As he slowly pulled his hands from her chest the void stopped where it was and her heart started to glow brighter and brighter but did not cover up her from like it normally would. The void started slowly inched back down her body to her feet as if to rebuild all it had taken. Taking in a deep gasp of air she sat up and looked him right in the eyes. The old laid was right. The catalyst was the key to everything.

"Welcome back my love," he said to her neither of them said anything more but came closer for a kiss.

Back in the real world the burning intensity of the light they were emanating caused the demon elf to block it with his arms. Not that id did any good as his flesh burned off and floated away in the wind. The howling screams of the demon as it died echoed out to all. Once the demon was dead Max and Garliva stopped glowing. Their lips still firmly pressed to one another.

"Aww that's just too damn cute," Came the voice of Dyronn. Pulling from the kiss the two looked over to see See him and Ragina smiling their way.

"Hell yeah," Jabber said as he walked over helping Max to his feet. "Y'know I always liked you right. That whole redneck stuff was just a joke. You know that right?"

"Yeah Jabber I know that. I also see you got yourself a white girl," Max teased.

"Yeah, but," he leaned in, "Keep that on tha down low hear? Don't need Ragina knowin' she'll never let me for get it, know what I'm sayin'?"

"Mmmmhmmm," came Ragina's voice as they both looked over to see her crossing her arms.

"Hey you did that to yourself," was all Annabelle said as she was walking off bouncing the baby on her hip. Jabber panicked walked after Ragina only to get her back the whole way. Laughing a bit he was met with Dyronn's pat on the shoulder. Garliva reached out taking his hand in her own smiling at him the whole time.

Lifting Max in a big hug the large dragon squeezed him tight, "I know you were the brood brother to save us. Were you go, we go," he said as he placed Max back on the ground. All the female dragons huddled around them scooting Garliva and Max closer together.

"We will all have the perfect brood," Szallsilic said while Klmakila came up behind Max wrapping her arms around his stomach.

"I want to be the first to bare his eggs," she added. Garliva hissed at Klmakila.

"I'm sorry girls, you can be part of the brood, but Garliva is the only one I want to be with. Looking up at the large dragon he continued, "I would be honored if you would be with my brood. They all want a family pretty bad,"

"For you anything," the large dragon said as she held out his arms, "So which of you ladies are first. All of them looked at Max. Smiling he pointed at Sazallsilic and then at Klmakila. Both became very excited as they both strolled off with the large dragon along with all the other lizard females. The officer and one of the glass wolves walked up to him.

"Well your name may not be Isaac, but I can call you friend," the officer said reaching out his hand to shake Max's in his own.

"I agree. If ever you need a pack to join. We glass wolves will always accept you as one of our own,"

"Thank you both," was all Max could say as they both watched the two nod to them and walk away.

"Now...where was I?" Max asked only to have Garliva reach up with her clawed finger and pull his chin her direction meeting their lips in a long and passionate kiss.

-The end

Made in the USA
Columbia, SC
08 December 2020

27074189R00096